POISON VALLEY

POISON VALLEY

by

Robert Eynon

Dales Large Print Books
Long Preston, North Yorkshire,
BD23 4ND, England.

British Library Cataloguing in Publication Data.

Eynon, Robert
    Poison Valley.

    A catalogue record of this book is
    available from the British Library

    ISBN   1-84262-304-4 pbk

First published in Great Britain in 2003 by Robert Hale Ltd.

Copyright © Robert Eynon 2003

Cover illustration © Michael Taylor by arrangement with
P.W.A. International Ltd.

Published in Large Print 2004 by arrangement with
Robert Hale Ltd.

Dales Large Print is an imprint of Library Magna Books Ltd.

Printed and bound in Great Britain by
T.J. (International) Ltd., Cornwall, PL28 8RW

Dedicated to
Jo and Lyn, Pete and Babs

ONE

The first thing that Billy Eason noticed about the stranger was his smile. It was playful and contagious, and it enhanced the classical handsomeness of his features. It was the sort of smile that would win most men over to his side, and maybe break the heart of a susceptible young lady.

The saloon was almost empty this early in the evening, except for a handful of old-timers who sat and dozed in what remained of the sultry afternoon heat. The newcomer walked stiffly over to the counter and deposited a silver dollar on the polished woodwork. When he came over to Eason's table he was carrying the cold beer the bartender had just served him.

'Mind if I join you, young feller?' he enquired, though he looked no more than a few years older than the cowboy himself. 'I've had a hard day's ride.'

The dust he brushed off his jacket told its own story, but the clothes he wore had a certain quality; whatever his occupation, the stranger was by no means a saddle bum. He took a long swig out of his glass, then replaced it on the table in front of him.

'My name's Luke,' he informed the cowboy. 'Luke Mathews.'

'Pleased to meet you, Luke,' Billy Eason said warily, without offering his hand. He liked friendly people, but he always bided his time rather than accept everyone on face value.

'Do you have a name?' Mathews asked. His smile was mischievous now, as if he was rebuking the cowboy for his caution.

'Billy – Billy Eason.'

'You live in this town?'

'Nope. I'm just passing through. I've been doing some cattle driving, but that came to an end in Cheyenne.'

As he was speaking, Mathews produced

three small eggcups from a pocket in his velvet jacket and inverted them on the table top alongside his glass. He then held up a nondescript brown button between his thumb and forefinger and announced:

'I'm gonna slide this button under one of the cups and shuffle them around a few times,' he told Eason. 'If you guess which one it's under when I've finished shuffling you'll earn yourself a dollar.'

The young cowboy watched his hands intently as they moved the eggcups in confusing circles. When the movements ceased he made his choice, but it was a bad one. When Mathews raised the cup he'd indicated it proved to be empty.

'Hard luck,' Mathews told him. 'Try again.'

He did, a dozen times, but with the same negative result. Finally, sensing the youngster's growing disappointment and frustration, the trickster seemed to relent. He held out a clenched fist, then unclenched it to reveal the brown button that had been tormenting Billy Eason.

'Take it,' he grinned. 'Buy yourself a drink, and get one for the bartender as well.'

The young cowboy felt his colour rising. He wasn't used to being taunted like this. Mathews closed his hand as he thrust it towards Billy Eason. Billy was about to brush it aside angrily when the fist opened again. By now the commonplace brown button had been turned into a shining dollar piece.

'Take it,' Mathews said again. 'It ain't gonna bite you!'

'I ain't so sure of that,' Eason mumbled, but Mathews was pressing the coin into his hand. 'Anyways, why are you buying me a drink? I ain't done nothing to earn it.'

'Sure you have,' the trickster replied. 'You've helped keep me sharp for when the customers get here, and it's always useful to have the bartender on your side if you're in a tight corner.'

The practice he'd had certainly seemed to work; as the saloon slowly filled up with evening customers, Luke Mathews was the centre of attraction with his fancy tricks. The eggcup trick brought them round him in droves. For ten cents a guess they had a chance to win a dollar by making the right choice as to the brown button's whereabouts. Occasionally one of them got it right, but not often enough to prevent Mathews's profits piling up. He only conceded the dollar prize when it was needed to revive the customers' interest in the trick.

When that stunt was exhausted as a moneyspinner Mathews took out a pack of cards and the menfolk paid willingly for the privilege of being bamboozled by his sleight of hand. Aces moved mysteriously through the pack, and at a sharp word of command the jack of clubs or the king of hearts would leap head-height from among its fellows and land face up on the table top in front of the astonished spectators.

Only one of the men in the saloon seemed to show any resentment at what was going on. He was a barrel-chested fellow with big arms and a bulging belly that betrayed a liking for his food and drink. At an early stage in the proceedings he chanced his luck twice and lost both times. After that he remained close to the trickster, watching his every movement in brooding silence.

Billy Eason didn't pay particular attention to the big man. The young cowboy was kept busy ferrying beers from the bar for himself and Luke Mathews. This type of conjuring seemed to be thirsty business because Mathews's glass was always empty. Billy was drinking much more than he was used to as well, since it was all paid for by the trickster who'd adopted him for the evening.

Then the good-natured jollities turned sour in a flash. The big man who'd been observing with such morbid fascination suddenly spoke out.

'Hey you, dude,' he said in a loud voice. 'Let's see that first trick of yours again.'

Luke Mathews stopped what he was doing and turned to face the man. 'D'you mean the ones with the cups?' he enquired.

'That's right; the one with the cups.'

Mathews duly set the cups and the button on the table.

'You got your ten cents ready?' he asked the big man.

'I'll pay if I lose,' the man said aggressively

'Okay,' Mathews replied mildly. 'And I'll pay if you win.'

The big man watched him as he shuffled the cups. He'd had plenty of time to think about what he was going to do.

'I'll take that one,' he said, pointing his finger, but it was the wrong choice once again.

'D'you want another try?' Luke Mathews asked him. 'Ten cents first.'

The big man's expression had turned even more surly.

'Keep your hands off them cups, dude,' he warned. 'There ain't no button under any of them, and I'm gonna prove it.'

'Go ahead,' the trickster invited him. 'Take a real close look.'

Standing nearby, Billy Eason had no idea

what was going to happen next. As the big man bent over the table to raise the remaining cups and take a closer look, Luke Mathews threw a sharp punch that flattened the big man's nose. Blood gushed out over the table and the fellow was stunned for a moment. Then he began to lumber forward, hitting the table over in his eagerness for revenge.

The crowd of men, who had been so happy a moment earlier, suddenly began to take sides in the dispute and a near riot began to develop. Because of the men punching and wrestling all around him Luke Mathews found himself hemmed in as the giant of a man advanced. Billy Eason pushed some men aside as he tried to get between his new-found friend and his assailant, but he too was brushed aside like a feather by one of the man's huge arms. Fuddled as he was by the beer he'd drunk, Billy foolishly drew his gun and held it up in front of the big man's face.

For a moment he thought the man was

going to try and eat the Colt .45, then the giant brought his head down sharply and caught the young cowboy a blow on the side of the temple. As he spun away under the force of the impact he felt an even sharper pain in his ribs. He looked round and saw that a law officer was standing there and that it was the barrel of the lawman's six-shooter that was causing this new discomfort.

A shot rang out and the fighting stopped almost immediately. Some plaster fell down from the ceiling where the bullet had embedded itself.

'Drop your gun, *now*,' the lawman hissed in Billy's ear and the Colt clattered to the floor.

There were three lawmen in the room by now: the town marshal who'd just fired the shot, the deputy who had Billy Eason covered and a second deputy standing in the doorway of the bar-room, holding a shotgun in his hands.

The marshal ignored the giant of a man who still had blood streaming from his nose.

He walked briskly over to where Luke Mathews and Billy were standing like statues.

'You're under arrest for disturbing the peace,' he informed the trickster. 'And you,' he added, addressing Billy Eason, 'for drawing a weapon in a public place.'

TWO

After they'd been dispossessed of their six-guns the two prisoners were escorted by the deputies to the township's jailhouse. It was only fifty yards or so along the main street, which explained how the lawmen had got to the scene in double quick time. Once inside the jailhouse, Billy Eason noticed that a game of cards had been in progress when the law officers had been called away to quell the riot in the saloon. One of the deputies led them over to the cells, while the other went over to the key rack on the wall behind the marshal's desk.

'They can share a cell,' he said, keys jangling in his hand. 'They don't seem to have no grievance against each other.'

The door swung open and Billy felt himself being propelled into the cell. Like the deputy said, he felt no grievance against anybody, not even against the men who'd arrested him. He was very drunk and even a prison bunk looked welcoming to him. He'd had a long day and felt like some shut-eye. He sprawled on to the straw mattress, gave a little sigh of contentment and promptly fell asleep.

Meanwhile, Luke Mathews had sat down on the other bunk and seemed to be deep in thought. The deputies paid no further attention to them, and went back to the card-game to await the town marshal's return.

When the marshal walked through the door of the jailhouse some ten minutes later, he was smiling broadly.

'Thanks for helping me out, fellers,' he said. 'Them deputy badges sure do suit you.'

The men laughed and Luke Mathews realized that they were merely friends of the lawman who'd been called from their card-game to help him sort out the trouble in the saloon.

'Wonder if that card-sharp feller would like to join our game?' the marshal went on. 'Maybe he can teach us a few tricks.'

Luke Mathews jumped at the chance; anything was better than spending the night cooped up in a cell. The lawman came and unlocked the door and let him out.

'Your partner looks kinda settled,' the marshal remarked. 'You wanna wake him?'

'He's just a kid,' Mathews replied. 'I don't think he's used to liquor. Best leave him sleep it off.'

They played well into the night until the marshal's two friends decided they'd had enough. Only then did Luke Mathews get some shut-eye. When he awoke the next morning he remembered that he'd won forty-seven dollars and a few cents during the game. To his surprise the money was still piled up on the lawman's desk, together with a couple of tin mugs of steaming black coffee.

'You'd better wake your partner now,' the marshal told him drily. 'This ain't no hotel, you know.'

A few minutes later Billy Eason was thankfully raising his mug to his parched lips. From what he could gather of the conversation, Mathews's winnings would be swallowed up by the fine for their misdemeanours of the previous evening. It came to fifty dollars, and the trickster handed over the balance rather regretfully.

Before they left the jailhouse the marshal scribbled out a note and handed it to Luke Mathews.

'What's this, a receipt?' Luke asked.

'Nope,' the lawman told him. 'It entitles you to a couple of breakfasts in Chiang's chop house along the street. It's my way of saying good riddance to you with a blessing!'

Although the food was good in the chop house, Billy Eason could only pick at it. Luke Mathews, on the other hand, tucked into everything with relish and even found room for what his young friend had left on his plate.

'I was right about the bartender,' Mathews announced with a touch of pride. 'He must have told the marshal we was OK; otherwise he'd have given us a rougher ride.'

Billy didn't comment; his mind and stomach were still in turmoil after the spree in the saloon.

'What you need is a stiff drink,' Luke said encouragingly. 'I gotta flask of bourbon in my saddle-bag over in the livery stable.'

The young cowboy's face turned even paler at the thought.

'No good?' Luke grinned. 'Well, drink as much water as you can take. It's gonna be a hot day.'

It wasn't until mid-afternoon that Billy Eason began to feel himself again, and to wonder what he was doing riding along with a card-sharp he hardly knew.

'Are we heading anywhere in particular?' he asked suddenly.

'The next town,' Luke told him. 'Anywhere I can make a pile.'

'What then?'

'I'm heading for Laramie,' Luke said. 'I ain't been there in a month of Sundays.

What about you?'

'I was thinking of heading south,' Billy replied. 'I'm told there's mining starting up in Colorado Territory. I ain't never tried it, but it cain't be much harder than cattle-driving.'

'God's own country, Colorado,' Luke remarked.

'You know it well?'

'I been there,' Luke said. 'I was in a place called Dos Santos. It's way south, past Denver.'

'I ain't ever heard of it,' Billy said.

'It's cattle country,' Luke told him. 'It gets dry and dusty in summer, but there's always some water coming down from the hills to the west. It was a small township, but maybe it's grown by now 'cos it ain't far from them hills, and that's where them mines will be if they're anywhere.'

'If I ever pass that way I'll take a look for myself,' Billy said. 'You still got friends there?'

Luke didn't speak for a moment. His

expression had turned quite serious as if his reminiscences had saddened him.

'There was a girl,' he said at last. 'She'll be in her late teens by now. Her name's Mary – Mary Stoller.'

Billy Eason smiled to lighten his partner's mood.

'If I ever do meet up with your Mary,' he asked, 'is there any message I can pass on for you?'

'Yeah, I guess there is,' Luke replied. 'Tell her that Luke is still alive and thinking about her all the time. Tell her I'll be back some day.'

Suddenly Billy had an idea.

'Why some day, Luke?' he said. 'Why not ride south with me?'

The card-sharp shook his head and spat dust on to the trail.

'The time ain't right,' he said. 'Besides, I gotta better idea.'

'What's that?'

'Ride as far as Laramie with me. We'll take in the townships along the way That way you'll have a stake to help you on your way south. I'll give you some money to take to Mary too, so's she'll know I ain't forgotten her.'

The young cowboy turned in his saddle and stared at his companion.

'You'd trust me with your money?' he asked incredulously. 'You don't hardly know me.'

'The money don't mean much,' Luke said. 'It's Mary I'd be trusting you with. You're a good-looking feller, Billy. I wouldn't want no harm to come to her, and no hurt either.'

'Why trust me, then?' Billy asked.

'Because of last night,' Luke said. 'You could have drifted away when the trouble started. Instead of that you stood by me. You even drew your gun, which could have got you killed.'

'I was drunk,' the young cowboy admitted.

'Maybe,' the card-sharp conceded. 'But I still appreciate it.'

He reined in his horse suddenly and dismounted.

'Get down,' he ordered, and his companion slid from his saddle.

'Drunk or not, that was a pretty smooth draw last night,' Luke said. 'Let's see if you can outdraw me, Billy. If I'm gonna be depending on you to watch my back, I wanna know how good you really are.'

Billy shrugged his shoulders.

'OK,' he agreed. 'What are we going to aim at?'

'Each other, of course.'

Billy's face registered surprise. His father had always warned him about fooling about with loaded guns. Luke Mathews read his thoughts.

'First we empty our guns,' he said.

Billy watched him take six shells out of the cylinder of his Colt .45 and drop them on the ground. The young cowboy unsheathed his gun and emptied it in the same fashion before replacing it in his holster. They stood facing each other, hands dangling near their belts.

'Your move,' the card-sharp told him. 'I'll

give you a chance.'

Both guns levelled simultaneously. Luke Mathews gave a short laugh. 'Let's try again,' he suggested.

They did, twice, each time with the same result. If there was a split second between them, it wasn't discernible.

'Guess we'd better call it quits,' Billy said. 'Otherwise we'll be here till nightfall. There ain't nothing in it.'

'Nothing my ass,' the gambler said sharply, as if his pride had been hurt. 'If this was for real you'd be a dead man by now.'

Billy Eason's face flushed crimson. He didn't like being called a liar, and it was the last thing he'd have expected of his amiable companion.

'I saw what I saw,' he retorted angrily. 'There ain't nothing between us.'

'And I know what I know,' Luke Mathews said. 'Now pick up them shells of yours, boy.'

Tight-lipped, the young cowboy stooped down to recover his bullets. Then he froze as a shot rang out, and one of the slugs was sent spinning along the ground away from his outstretched hand. He turned his head and looked up. Luke Mathews was holding a smoking gun in his hand, the same gun Billy had seen him empty of shells a moment or so earlier.

'Like you said, kid,' the gambler said, sheathing the Colt as he spoke, 'you saw what you saw. But me, I know what I know....'

THREE

The next five or six weeks were the most exciting and incident-filled that cowboy Billy Eason had ever lived through. Wherever they went Luke Mathews was the centre of attention. Townsfolk and countryfolk alike flocked in droves to watch his conjuring tricks or to accept his challenge to a game of blackjack or poker.

Such was the gambler's personality that he and Billy made friends in every place they visited, be it lone farmhouse or bustling township. Of course, they made some enemies as well along the way, but very few, which was surprising considering the ease with which Luke Mathews parted people from their hard-earned money.

Maybe Luke's secret was that he always had a smile on his face, and his jokes and stories took the sting out his opponents' losses. Many of the folk they met led lives of drudgery on a few acres of soil. Luke had lived and travelled extensively, and his anecdotes of the world beyond were like revelations of another planet.

As for Billy, he just couldn't believe how easy it was to make money without working for it. It came in so fast that Luke could afford to stand rounds of drinks for all and sundry yet still add profit to their saddlebags at the end of most days.

'You should be banking some of this money, Luke,' the cowboy advised his partner one day, but Luke Mathews just grinned at him.

'Banking my ass,' the gambler replied, using his favourite term of derision. 'If I'd banked money in half the places I been to, I'd spend the rest of my life on the trail trying to recover it.'

And all the time they drank, sometimes heavily. At first Billy tried to hold back, but the many hours they spent in drinking-houses eventually broke down his resolve. At first, he suffered badly after every boisterous spree, but in time his headaches grew less intense and his stomach seemed to harden to the lethal mixtures of beer and spirits he poured into it. Gradually his taste developed for the harder liquors and he only drank a cold beer at the hottest time of day. Besides, beer made him feel heavy and sluggish whereas whiskey gave him the impression of being sharp and alert to his surroundings.

And then there were the saloon girls; they weren't the type of women you'd want to take home to meet your folks, but after a few drinks their rouged lips and powdered cheeks looked irresistibly alluring. Occasionally they'd come across a troupe of dancing girls working their way township by township to the west coast. Both the gambler and his younger companion were attractive to women and each of them found no difficulty winning the favours of a different girl each evening.

'There ain't no sense sticking to one girl,' Luke Mathews advised the cowboy. 'It might give her the wrong idea regarding your intentions. That's when they start hanging around making a nuisance of themselves, squabbling with other women and telling everyone what a lousy rat you are. And don't start getting over-fond of one of them neither, 'cause that can give you even more problems.'

In his idle moments, watching the gambler exercising his charms so effectively on the opposite sex, Billy Eason tried to picture in his mind what kind of girl Mary Stoller could be – the girl Luke Mathews had left behind in Dos Santos, Colorado. She must be very beautiful, he reasoned, for Luke to keep her memory alive for so many years. She was probably virtuous, too; if she'd been too easy a conquest the gambler would have long forgotten her, as he forgot most of the women he enjoyed on his travels.

He'd have liked to learn more about her from his partner, but he'd quickly realized that any mention of Dos Santos brought a mixed reaction of pleasure and pain to the gambler.

Laramie had changed radically since Luke Mathews's last visit. As he and Billy Eason rode into the town he noted that the higgledy-piggledy tin shanties that had sprung up to house the men who'd constructed the railroad through Laramie on its way to the west coast had been replaced by more permanent wooden buildings. It was a growing township but it was by no means a boomtown. The hard-working, hard-drinking types he'd encountered on his previous visit had long since moved on with the railroad. In those bustling days pickings had been easy for a card-sharp. Now he'd have to make his money from the settled residents of the town, who had wives to go home to and families to support. It was going to be harder, less lucrative work.

So he knuckled down to the task, with Billy Eason propping up the bar near at hand in case of trouble. One evening that was much like any other Billy was watching his partner playing dice at a nearby table. Throwing dice was not Luke's favourite sport, as it relied too much on chance. However, he'd entered this particular game in the hope that the players would eventually tire of the game and produce a pack of cards instead.

The swing-doors of the saloon opened suddenly and two dusty riders walked stiffly into the room. They were tall, lean men with elongated faces and prominent teeth that gave them a horsey look. They were similar enough in features to be brothers, though they were separated by four or five years in age.

When they reached the counter they demanded a bottle of whiskey and two glasses. They emptied their first drink in one gulp, then leaned against the bar, watching the game of dice a few yards away from where they were standing.

'That feller sitting there,' one of them said

to his companion. 'Ain't that Luke from our old outfit?'

The words had been spoken too quietly to travel as far as the table where Luke was sitting, but Billy Eason heard them well enough. He sidled a little closer to the two men, who were both watching the gambler intently

'It sure could be, Marv,' the younger man agreed. 'But it's a long time since I last saw him, and I always remember him with a moustache.'

Billy pushed his glass away from him. He didn't know what the strangers had in common with his friend, but he did know that he ought to refrain from drinking too heavily for the moment. They could turn out to be old buddies of Luke; on the other hand they might be carrying a grudge against the card-sharp.

Whatever their feelings about Luke, Billy didn't like the look of them. They were shifty-eyed and talked out of the sides of their mouths as if they were constantly sharing secrets.

Billy merely kept the men under observation for the time being, but when he saw that Luke's glass was empty he picked up a bottle of rye from the counter and walked casually over to the gambler's table. As he stooped over Luke's shoulder to pour him a drink he muttered a few words to apprise him of the presence of the strangers at the bar.

For a few minutes the gambler seemed to pay no attention to the information he'd been given; then he glanced nonchalantly towards the corner of the bar where the newcomers were standing. By now Billy Eason was ready for any eventuality; the liquor he'd consumed had made him aggressive at the slightest hint of danger to his benefactor, and as he watched Marv and his companion he kept his hand dangling near the butt of his Colt .45.

Fortunately, after a couple of seconds Luke Matthews's face broke into a smile of recognition.

'Marv Richards,' he said, rising from the table as he spoke. 'Where you been keeping yourself? Ain't that your young brother Danny?'

The elder brother returned his smile with a lopsided leer that seemed to cut his face in half, and he accepted the hand that Luke Matthews offered him. But when the gambler turned towards the younger brother, Danny almost recoiled against the wooden counter.

'You ain't got no toad in your hand, have you, Luke?' he enquired sharply. 'No spider? I cain't never forget them tricks you used to play on me.'

The card-sharp laughed out loud and turned over his palm to reveal that it was quite empty.

'Me play a trick like that on you, Danny?' he said. 'Never in a thousand years!'

'Danny's grown up some since them days,' Marv Richards informed him. 'He's got a temper on him, too, so you'd better go easy on him, Luke.'

Billy glanced across at Danny, whom he took to be a couple of years older than himself. Danny's face was set like stone, as if he had a long memory and didn't intend to be trifled with further. As for Luke, he didn't seem at all put out by the warning.

'Them was bad old days,' he reminded the brothers. 'I guess I just had to fool around like that to keep my sanity.'

Neither man made any comment, but the gambler slapped Marv Richards playfully on the back.

'Anything I did to annoy you fellers in the past, I'm sorry for,' he told them. 'I'm gonna make up for it tonight. Whatever you boys can drink is going straight on to my bill.'

And drink they did, reminiscing all the time about the past when they'd all been in the same army unit in the Civil War. When they'd finished talking about the war they turned to recounting their adventures since the demise of the Southern cause.

Much of what was said went over Billy

Eason's head. Now that he had no more fears about the strangers' intentions he let himself go and by the end of the evening he was sagging in his chair. He vaguely remembered being helped upstairs to the room he shared with Luke Mathews. Next morning he woke up fully clothed on his bed. At the far end of the room Luke was still snoring; raucously. Billy closed his eyes again and drifted back into slumber.

He opened his eyes as his partner playfully splashed water down on to his face.

'We gotta be going,' the gambler told him. 'I'm meeting Marvin and Danny at noon or thereabouts.'

'Where's that?' the young cowboy enquired. 'Here in town?'

'Nope,' Luke replied. 'They're camped in a canyon east of Laramie. They drew us a map. Don't you remember?'

As Billy pulled himself to his feet a terrible pain shot through his head.

'I need water,' he said plaintively. 'God, what a night!'

As it turned out, neither of them was in much shape to hit the trail before noon. In the course of what remained of the morning the gambler filled his young partner in regarding the conversation of the night before.

'Marv and Danny are on their way to meet up with some more old buddies of mine in Cheyenne,' Luke informed him. 'I cain't miss out on a chance like that, Billy, so I'm gonna team up with them for a while.'

The news made Billy feel even more downcast. Despite the heavy drinking they'd done together, he still couldn't take to the two brothers. There was something about them he didn't trust. Luke Mathews seemed to read his mind.

'What's wrong, Billy'?' he asked. 'You're welcome to ride with us. Don't you want to?'

The cowboy hesitated; even thinking made his head sore.

'I guess not, Luke,' he said at last. 'I reckon I'll head south, like I been planning to. If you're meeting up with old friends there ain't no need for me to tag along.'

One or two of the residents waved goodbye to them as they rode out of town. In the short time they'd been there the folk of Laramie had taken them to their hearts. As usual, Luke Mathews had breezed in and out of the township like a breath of fresh air.

They'd been riding for about half an hour when the gambler consulted the map for the first time.

'I guess this is where I turn off,' he told his partner. 'If Marv's got it right, they're camped out about a mile from here along that trail.'

As they'd been told, the trail led into a forbidding-looking canyon. As the gambler let his gaze wander over the surroundings Billy Eason dismounted and began to open one of his saddlebags.

'What are you doing now?' the gambler asked him.

'Giving you your money back,' Billy replied. 'I ain't done nothing to earn it. I just been holding it for you.'

'Holding my ass!' Luke commented, forcing a smile to his lips despite his sadness at losing the young cowboy's company. 'Like I said, that's your stake for the future, Billy. And hang on a second; I got a hundred dollars here that I want you to take to that girl I told you about, Mary Stoller.'

He brushed aside all the youngster's objections and counted out the money.

'Ain't many fellers I'd trust like this,' he added solemnly. 'Don't let me down.'

'Why d'you need to meet up with them Richards brothers?' Billy asked suddenly, 'Why cain't you just ride to Cheyenne alone?'

'You don't like them, do you, Billy?' Luke remarked.

'Not much,' the cowboy admitted. 'I don't trust them.'

'But I do,' Luke said. 'I saved Marv Richards's life once, like other buddies saved mine. If you ain't been in a war, you cain't understand things like that, Billy.'

'You talked a lot last night,' the young cowboy reminded him. 'I don't remember everything that was said, but I know you were talking about how well you'd been doing. I just hope you're doing the right thing, that's all.'

'I'm doing the right thing, Billy,' Luke assured him, and then they shook hands. 'Look after yourself, and be good,' he added with a wink.

Instead of heading south immediately, Billy Eason stood and watched rider and horse pick their way along the narrow, stony trail leading into the canyon. It was level for the first few hundred yards, rose quite steeply for a while and then seemed to descend again as it disappeared behind one of the jaws of the canyon.

Billy reached for his canteen and took a deep swig. His head still felt lousy from the drink. When he looked up again, Luke Mathews had passed out of sight, leaving the cowboy with a strange empty feeling after so many weeks of the card-sharp's boisterous companionship. Even now he hesitated about what to do next. It still wasn't too late to change his mind and follow the gambler to the rendezvous with the Richards brothers.

Then a shot echoed within the canyon walls and sent a pair of buzzards soaring into the cloudless sky, screeching protests against whoever had broken the silence of their domain.

Billy pressed his hand to his temple as a host of fears and imaginings crowded into his fuddled brain. There might be an innocent explanation for the gunfire: a shot let off in high spirits, maybe, or the chance to bag some game for supper. However, he knew he couldn't just ride away from the place with doubt in his mind. He had to go and check that his friend was okay.

He decided to leave his mare at the entrance to the canyon. If he encountered trouble there was hardly room to turn a horse around on the narrow trail; and if the mare panicked it could injure itself and he'd have to walk all the way back to Laramie carrying his possessions.

He made his way into the canyon as quickly as he could, but he found the gradient hard on his lungs and legs. He'd been burning the candle for weeks and the excessive drinking of the previous evening had knocked the stuffing out of him. He was relieved when the trail began to descend again.

His first glimpse inside the canyon basin confirmed his worst fears: a hundred yards or so away, and some forty feet below him, lay the spread-eagled body of Luke Mathews. It was lying at a grotesque angle, like a discarded marionette, and from the position of the head Billy guessed that the fall or the bullet had broken the gambler's neck.

He realized that he too was vulnerable and he hugged the shade of the nearest large boulder. Everything was still in the canyon, too still. Had he been spotted? Was the dry-gulcher waiting for him to re-emerge into the sunlight? His stomach muscles were knotted with anxiety and his head throbbed painfully. There was nothing he could do for his former partner; he had to save his own skin now. He dropped into a crouch and scrambled back the way he'd come. It was only when the trail dropped out of sight of the canyon basin that he straightened up again and ran headlong down the slope to the safety of his horse.

He was barely in the saddle when a second shot rang out in the canyon. A shiver ran through Billy Eason's body as he pictured the killer pressing a gun against Luke's head to finish him off, or maybe the gambler's horse had been injured and was being put out of its misery Either way, he'd never know the answer but if he'd been spotted there was a fair chance that the killer would want to pursue him and silence him, so Billy galloped off southwards as if he had a posse of devils on his tail.

FOUR

As Billy Eason rode deep into Colorado
Territory he couldn't lose the sense of guilt
that obsessed him. If only he'd gone along
like his partner had suggested, maybe Luke
Mathews would still be alive. Why had he
abandoned him like that, after everything
the gambler had done for him? Why hadn't
he traded shots with the dry-gulcher who'd
taken his friend's life? Why had he run away
like a startled jack-rabbit?

It didn't help that his saddle-bag was full of
dollars that Luke had given him; if he'd been
destitute he couldn't have afforded to keep
on drinking. As it was he had money to burn
and liquor seemed the only release he had
from the nightmare of guilt. Of course, like
most drunks Billy couldn't face the fact that
drink was a major cause of his problems; if

he'd only sobered up for a while, maybe he'd have found the strength to confront reality and solve his predicament.

Not all his feelings towards his former partner were motivated by grief. When he was feeling sorry for himself he cursed his partner for not revealing the secret of some of his tricks. At least they could have helped him make a living in the saloons which had become his habitat. But Luke had been adamant about that.

'It's my livelihood,' the gambler had explained on more than one occasion. 'My tricks are something I just got to keep close to my chest.'

'You selfish sonofabitch,' Billy would mutter to nobody in particular now that the card-sharp was dead. 'You never did give a damn about nobody else, Luke.'

But then he'd remember his friend's openness and generosity and tears would well up in his eyes. That's when the other customers pointed him out and sniggered at him behind his back. Just another saddle bum who couldn't hold his liquor.

By the time he reached Denver his bankroll had dwindled alarmingly. He tried to retrieve the situation at the gaming tables, but that was a disaster. When he left Denver all he had left was the hundred dollars Luke Mathews had asked him to deliver to the girl the cowboy had never met, Mary Stoller. He managed somehow to bum his way through the next couple of townships on his way south without dipping into that reserve.

But he couldn't put the inevitable off for ever. Eventually he was forced to sell his last friend, his mare. The subsequent depression he suffered made him hit the bottle with even more abandon. Now there was no thought for Mary Stoller or for anybody; he drank the dregs left by other customers or picked up their drinks up when he thought they weren't looking. One evening he tried to walk out of a saloon with a bottle of bourbon he hadn't paid for. Only the timely arrival of the town marshal saved him from a beating at the hands of the burly bartender, but it also got him another night in the town jail.

The next morning he was roughly shaken from his deep slumber by the deputy marshal.

'Get a move on,' the lawman ordered. 'You're leaving town.'

Billy Eason blinked up at him, and tried to focus his thoughts. If he had to go on foot, how long would it take him to reach the nearest town or settlement?

'I can't just go,' he protested. 'I ain't got a horse.'

'There's a coach heading south,' the deputy informed him. 'It's just across the street. You're taking it.'

The cowboy let himself be tugged to his feet, but he hadn't given up the argument.

'I cain't ride no stage,' he whined. 'I ain't got a cent.'

'You're gonna earn your passage for once,' the lawman told him brusquely.

'The feller riding shotgun took sick in the

51

night. You're taking his place, so get over to that pitcher of water and try to clean up a bit. There's a young lady travelling on the stage, and you ain't a pretty sight!'

There were three people standing near the stagecoach on the opposite side of the main street. They had rested overnight on the upper floor of the saloon, and now they were happy to stretch their legs a little before the day's journey began. One of the men was formally dressed in a dark suit, starched shirt and tie as if he was planning to spend a day in the office rather than on a hot, dusty stagecoach. The other man was casually dressed and his Colt .45 hung low on his hip. If the first man had the confident air of a successful businessman, his companion conveyed the easy nonchalance of a seasoned gunslinger.

The third member of the group was the young lady the lawman had spoken of. Still in her late teens, she was slight but shapely and her rich blonde hair tumbled on to her shoulders, enhancing even further the natural beauty of her features.

The businessman turned to speak to her.

'We should be home by late afternoon, Mary,' he told her. 'It's less of a haul than yesterday's journey.'

He was smiling at her in a fatherly, yet lascivious way. He must have been twice her age but he was obviously working hard to impress her. The gunslinger was watching them with a sardonic smile on his lips. The girl meant nothing to him; his job was to protect Matt Lawson, attorney at law in the growing township of Dos Santos. Everything else on the journey was a matter of indifference to him.

The girl murmured a couple of phrases about the previous day's travel, just to stop Lawson staring at her in that way. She was rather overawed by the company of the two men, neither of whom she liked very much. The lawyer turned his attention away from her momentarily.

'Sheldon, did you bring Mary's luggage down?' he enquired of the gunslinger, who nodded his head almost imperceptibly.

'The coach driver's loading it on right now,' he confirmed.

'Thank you, Mr Darch,' the young lady said politely but without warmth. 'I'm sorry it's so heavy. My aunt insisted on weighing me down with presents for myself and my father.'

'It wasn't heavy at all,' Darch replied in a bored voice and then spat in the dust at their feet.

The lawyer took advantage of the ensuing silence to renew his conversation with the beautiful girl.

'It's quite a coincidence our being in Denver at the same time,' he remarked. 'You visiting your aunt, and me conducting important business for Loyd Gubby.'

The girl didn't reply; in fact, she wasn't even looking at him. She was watching a young fellow who'd just come out of the door of the local jail and was making his way across the street to where the stagecoach stood waiting. The cowboy's gait was unsteady as if he was ill or something, and he wasn't wearing a badge. Besides, he looked far too unkempt to be a lawman, she thought.

As he drew closer she was strangely unsettled by the intensity of his eyes and his rugged good looks, despite the fact that his face was pale and drawn and there was a few days' stubble on his chin.

Matt Lawson turned to see what it was that had robbed him of the girl's attention. When his eyes alighted on the shabby stranger his lips parted in a contemptuous sneer.

'Don't let that feller over there worry you, Mary,' he told the girl. 'If he comes too close, Sheldon will send him packing.'

It wasn't fear that the girl was experiencing but fascination. As the stranger hesitated when he reached the coach, their eyes met for a moment and she felt her heart miss a beat. Then she heard the coach driver's voice.

'Are you the young feller who's gonna ride shotgun?'

Billy Eason turned and looked up to where the driver was strapping down the last item of luggage.

'I ... I guess so,' he replied in a quiet voice, as if he was unsure of himself.

'Speak up, son,' the driver told him. 'My hearing ain't what it used to be. You got a name?'

'Eason, Billy Eason.' The voice was stronger now, and the girl found it very pleasant to listen to.

'Well, help the young lady on to the coach, Eason,' the driver instructed him. 'I'm just about finished up here. Sooner we leave the better.'

After less than half an hour on the trail Billy had already heard most of the stage driver's life history. The man's name was Henry but from Kentucky to New Mexico he was known as Harry Hotspur, a name which he reckoned was borrowed from some English king or other, but which Henry had earned for himself while working as a rider for the Pony Express. He was in

56

his fifties now and had lost almost all his teeth in fist-fights and accidents connected with his profession.

'Broke lots of bones, too,' he confided proudly to his young companion. 'You see, son, Hotspur ain't the kind of feller who gives in, whatever the odds.'

Despite his joviality, Henry was disappointed at the lack of response he was getting from the youngster to his stories.

'What's wrong, son?' he enquired at last. 'Are you travel-sick or something?'

The cowboy gave a wry smile.

'Just sick, I reckon,' he replied honestly. 'I drank too much last night. I was kinda hoping to sleep late this morning, at the marshal's expense.'

The stage driver grinned broadly.

'It ain't sleep you need, son,' he said, 'but another drink. We'll stop to water the horses at the next arroyo we come to, then I'll get my flask of rye whiskey out. Never do go far without my flask of rye,' he added with a mischievous twinkle in his eye.

The passengers took the opportunity to stretch their limbs while the horses partook of the cool liquid of the arroyo. Lawyer Matt Lawson was not in the best of moods; the girl was proving even less communicative than on the previous day. It was as if her mind was on other things.

Gunslinger Sheldon Darch had the situation pretty well figured out, and it amused him to watch Lawson soft-soaping the girl for hours on end while the object of her thoughts was sitting somewhere above their heads. Maybe the lawyer had an inkling of the truth as well, because during their break from the coach he ushered the girl away from the rest of the group.

'Let's take a little stroll, my dear,' he told her. 'It's good to move about after a long spell in the coach.'

Although Billy Eason found the girl very beautiful, he couldn't wait for her and the rest of the passengers to pass out of sight inside the coach. When he heard the door slam he made a grab for the tin flask Henry offered him.

'Hey, steady on.' The driver rebuked him with mock severity. 'That flask's got to last us both till we hit Dos Santos.'

At the sound of the name Billy drew the flask from his lips. For him the words had an ominous ring to them. He felt an almost physical pain in his gut as he recalled the commission Luke Mathews had given him, and the hundred dollars he'd squandered along the way.

'Dos Santos?' he said. 'Is that where we're heading?'

'That's where these folks get off,' Henry confirmed. 'But you can stay on till the end of the line if you like, young feller. That's if you ain't had enough of my company already.'

By mid-afternoon Billy Eason was feeling much better, though his eyes betrayed the influence of the rye he'd consumed. He and the driver were getting along like old buddies and they were both very relaxed. Meanwhile the sun was casting ever longer shadows as the stage climbed the gradient of the last pass before Dos Santos.

'After this climb it's plain sailing,' Henry informed his companion. 'There's still fifteen miles or so to cover but it's all downhill or flat country.'

The young cowboy at his side didn't really care. He was starting to feel drowsy in spite of the constant shaking of the coach. He'd already made up his mind to stay on the stage as long as possible. He was broke but the driver was a good sort who wouldn't see him starve. Maybe there was a future for him in this sort of life; at least it would keep him out of the saloons while he was working.

They had almost reached the crest of the pass when a man on horseback appeared suddenly from behind a large boulder. He was holding a sixgun in his hand and as they approached he called out to them in a loud voice:

'Hold it there, mister. There's more of us further on, and they all got itchy fingers.'

It took a moment or two for Billy to realize that the stage was being held up. Luckily, Henry's reactions were much sharper.

'Use the gun, Billy,' he yelled into his companion's ear. 'Use the goddamned gun!'

At the same time he began urging the horses into a gallop. As the stage lurched forward and gathered speed one of its wheels caught the edge of a boulder. The coach lurched to one side and the shotgun went off unexpectedly in Billy Eason's hands, scaring the horses even further.

As the coach careered wildly over the crest and began the descent Billy was forced to drop the shotgun and try to grab on to a rail for support. He failed to make it; the next moment he was tumbling from the stage on to the hard earth below. Stunned by the fall he heard firing and the sound of horses' hoofs passing close by. Men were shouting and swearing but gradually all the sounds of the stagecoach and its pursuers faded into the distance.

Inside the coach the young lady had to

hang on for dear life to the person at her side, lawyer Matt Lawson. Lawson was scared too, but the desire to impress the beautiful girl made him suppress his fear.

'There, there, my dear,' he told her soothingly as she clung to him. 'Everything's going to be all right.'

Meanwhile, Sheldon Darch had poked his head out of the open window of the coach. There was firing coming from behind them, but not a fusillade. He guessed that they were up against no more than a couple of pursuers – three at the most. Darch had been up against worse odds than these, and he had a cool head in a fight. As long as that crazy driver of theirs didn't get hit, they had every chance of making it. He drew his Colt .45 and bided his time.

Eventually his patience paid off; as the coach veered round a bend one of the pursuers came into sight. There had been no hostile fire from the stage so far and the outlaws were growing confident – too confident. The rider was quite close and he and his mount presented a large target.

Darch opened fire with the Colt and brought the horse down with his third shot. A few moments later Harry Hotspur was whooping with triumph. The outlaws had given up the chase; they'd made it.

Back at the pass Billy Eason ran his fingers gingerly over the parts of his body that ached to check if any bones were broken. He couldn't believe how his luck had taken another turn for the worse. A short while ago he'd been dreaming of a career with a stagecoach company, and now he was licking his wounds in the middle of nowhere.

He didn't have much time to dwell on his misfortune. It wasn't long before he heard a horse approaching. As it came into view he saw that it was carrying two men on its back, and Billy sensed from the expression of the fellow holding the reins that they were not the bearers of good tidings. The horse halted about twenty yards from where the young cowboy was standing, and the second outlaw dismounted awkwardly.

As the man walked towards him Billy could see that he was limping badly. If anything he looked even angrier than his partner who'd remained in the saddle.

'So you're the sonofabitch who got my horse killed,' he snarled.

Billy wiped the sweat from his brow with his left hand; he could think of nothing to say.

'Don't kill him straightaway,' the mounted outlaw said suddenly. 'Let's make the varmint suffer.'

Billy Eason could sense that death was only about fifteen yards away, and he wasn't going to let it get any closer. The man facing him went for his gun nonchalantly confident of the odds and scornful of the youth and inexperience of his opponent. It was a bad mistake; Billy was a cornered animal and he reacted like one. He drew smoothly and shot the outlaw clean through the chest.

The other outlaw also had his gun drawn;

he let off a shot in Billy's direction but the horse under him wouldn't hold steady in the midst of all the excitement. Before the rider could fire a second time a slug from the cowboy's Colt doubled him up like a jackknife. He slid from the saddle on to the dusty trail and Billy watched the life-blood drain quickly from the gaping wound in his belly.

When the outlaws' bodies had finally stopped twitching, the young cowboy seemed to wake from a dream. He'd never killed a man before, and he celebrated the occasion by vomiting against the nearest boulder.

FIVE

There was a handful of townsfolk waiting outside the Mountain View saloon when the stagecoach reached Dos Santos. Pastor Stoller could tell from the saliva on the horses' necks that they'd been driven very hard. He was very much looking forward to being reunited with his daughter Mary, but when the girl emerged from the coach he was dismayed by the lack of colour in her cheeks and by the way she seemed to rely heavily on lawyer Matt Lawson to help her down. Mary was by nature a cheerful, bright-eyed young lady but now she looked serious and tense.

Loyd Gubby's hired gun Sheldon Darch was the last to leave the coach. The pastor didn't even spare him a glance as he hurried over to his daughter's side. Meanwhile,

Mary was staring up at Henry, the driver, and she didn't seem to comprehend what she saw.

'Where's the other one,' she asked in a bewildered voice, 'the one who was riding next to the driver?'

Matt Lawson moved even closer to her side, though his wife Beatrice had been standing there for half an hour in the afternoon heat to welcome him back.

'Yes, what's happened to the young fellow?' he demanded in a loud voice; he was anxious to express his solidarity with the young lady who cast such a spell on him, though personally he couldn't give a damn what had happened to Billy Eason.

Feeling all eyes upon him, Henry shifted uncomfortably on his seat.

'He let off the shotgun when them outlaws attacked us,' he informed them, 'and then he kinda toppled off the stage.'

Mary raised her hand to her mouth.

'Was ... was he hit?' she asked in a tremulous voice.

'I cain't say, miss,' the coach driver replied. 'Either way, there was nothing I could do about it. I had my hands full keeping the horses going.'

Pastor Stoller glanced at Sheldon Darch, who was calmly rolling a smoke. The gunslinger had caught a glimpse of the cowboy when he fell but he didn't deem it important enough to mention. Drunks like that were a dime a dozen in the West.

By this time Mary Stoller was quite distraught.

'But we must do something,' she exclaimed. 'We can't just leave him at the mercy of those outlaws.'

A hard-faced man was standing in the doorway of the saloon. When he caught Sheldon Darch's eye he indicated with a slight movement of the head that the gunslinger's presence was required inside the saloon. Darch understood that his employer Loyd Gubby, who owned the Mountain View saloon, wanted to talk to him. But as the hired gun made for the sidewalk, Mary Stoller reached out and grabbed his arm.

'Mr Darch,' she said pleadingly, 'you will go back to look for him, won't you?'

Darch turned to face her, unmoved by her youth and beauty.

'Nope, I won't,' he told her bluntly. 'Because I'm thirsty and he's dead.'

Her hand fell away from his arm and he continued on his way into the saloon. She looked up at the stagecoach driver, but he averted his gaze. Sure, he'd liked the young fellow and had shared his flask with him, but the gunfighter was right. Henry had a commission to carry out, and it didn't include going back into hostile country to recover a corpse.

Finally, the girl turned to the remaining passenger for support.

'Mr Lawson,' she said, 'that cowboy fired the shot that may have saved us all. Don't you see that it's wicked to turn our backs on him?'

The lawyer was embarrassed by her

persistence. What could he do? He wasn't a man of action like Sheldon Darch.

'I'm sorry, Mary,' he said lamely. 'I've got to report to Mr Gubby concerning our transactions in Denver.'

Only then did he turn and address his wife, whom he hadn't even embraced.

'You go on home, dear,' he told her. 'I shan't be long.'

At last Mary and her father were left alone, since the stage driver also had adjourned to the bar of the saloon to celebrate his escape from the outlaws.

'Don't worry, Mary,' Pastor Stoller said comfortingly. 'If you feel that strongly about it, we'll go and have a word with the town marshal.'

When the two hired guns came through the swing doors, their boss Loyd Gubby was standing at the window watching the people gathered around the stagecoach.

'You stay here, Corbett,' the saloon-owner said. 'When Lawson manages to tear himself away from the preacher's daughter tell him to join me and Darch in my office.'

Darch followed him over to a door near the foot of the wide, richly carpeted staircase. The gunslinger closed the door behind them as Gubby went and sat behind a mahogany table which was laden with paperwork. Darch wasn't invited to sit down, and didn't expect to be; the gunslinger knew his place.

Loyd Gubby was one of the few men Sheldon Darch respected. Though still only in his early thirties, Gubby had managed to get rich in the bruising free-for-all that followed the Civil War. Gubby never spoke about how he'd made his money, but his ruthless and single-minded nature must have helped. He was stocky and muscular though he no longer had to work hard physically, but it was his sharp brain that provided the cutting edge. His goal at the moment was to become the most prominent citizen in the territory and he was well on the way to achieving it.

'What was all the fuss about?' he enquired as he lit a cigar. 'What was the Stoller girl getting all het up about?'

Darch related the story in a detached tone of voice. For many folk the attempted hold-up would have been the experience of a lifetime, but to Darch it was all in a day's work. He didn't even bother to emphasize his own role in foiling the outlaws' plans.

'What do you know about the young feller you lost?' Gubby asked. 'What was he to the girl?'

'Nothing,' the hired gun replied. 'I don't think he even noticed her. He was just a drunk with a good-looking face that she took a fancy to.'

He couldn't understand his employer's interest in the two youngsters; but interested he was, without a doubt.

'What do you mean a *drunk?*' the saloon-owner persisted. 'You mean he was drinking on the stage?'

'Maybe that too,' Darch commented. 'But by the look of him he'd been drinking for days, maybe months. The stage driver only took him on board because the usual feller took sick.'

Loyd Gubby found the situation ironic. He'd invested a lot of money in this township, buying up this and that when it became available, but he hadn't managed to win the affection of the inhabitants. Pastor Stoller in particular had little good to say about the malign influence of 'certain outsiders' in his weekly sermons. Yet here was the man of God's only daughter falling for a saddle bum who couldn't hold his liquor, or even on to the rail of the stagecoach he was riding. He wondered what it took to become a folk hero!

Sheldon Darch waited for his boss to move on to another subject; instead, Gubby lapsed into a silence the gunslinger found irritating. He'd much rather be outside in the barroom, enjoying a cold beer with the boys.

There was a respectful knock on the door, and then lawyer Matt Lawson poked his head inside.

'Excuse me, Loyd,' he said in a deferential tone of voice. 'Corbett told me you were ready to see me.'

'That's right,' the saloon-owner confirmed. 'By the way I hear you had some excitement on the way back.'

The lawyer was glad Gubby had raised the subject; he didn't feel comfortable about the way he'd turned his back on the lovely young girl outside the saloon.

'Miss Stoller is rather concerned about the fate of the young fellow who fell from the stagecoach,' he said, then took a deep breath before continuing. 'She ... she thinks that something should be done about it.'

At this point his voice faltered a little; he didn't wish to appear to be giving orders to Gubby and Darch. The saloon owner didn't seem at all put out, however.

'Me and Darch were just talking about the same thing,' Gubby said. 'Darch is going back to see how the young hero's faring.'

The lawyer was surprised by Gubby's reaction, but not half as surprised as Sheldon Darch. The saloon-owner warmed to the theme.

'You can take your pardners Corbett and Stiles,' he told the gunslinger. 'Do you reckon the three of you can handle it, or shall I wake Marshal Stevens up to keep you company?'

Realizing that it wasn't a joke but a command, Sheldon Darch applied his mind to the task ahead.

'Three of us will be enough,' he assured his boss. 'From what I could see, the fellers who attacked the stage were a bunch of amateurs. They couldn't break into a bank with no walls. But if you expect us to bring the cowboy back alive, forget it. He'll be meat for the crows by now.'

'Well, at least you'll have tried,' the saloon-owner commented philosophically. 'And it might even get us a favourable mention in next Sunday's sermon. By the way, don't forget to call in at the jailhouse to let the marshal know what you're doing, and make sure that plenty of folk see you leave Dos Santos with a spare horse in tow. The more publicity we get out of this, the better.'

SIX

Town Marshal Stevens never thought the day would come when he'd welcome a visit from a trio of undesirables like Darch, Corbett and Stiles; but now he had to admit that their presence was a welcome relief from the uncomfortable ten minutes he'd just spent in the company of Pastor Stoller and his daughter Mary.

Stevens had already turned fifty and he could look back with pride on a long career of solid, if unspectacular lawkeeping. Things had changed a lot since the end of the Civil War, with a boom in mining in the surrounding hills and a consequent growth in farming and ranching on the vast expanses of plains that spread eastwards from Dos Santos.

Expansion was good news for the townspeople, but not for Stevens. More residents and more visitors, miners and cowboys, meant a lot more problems for a lawman, and Stevens was starting to feel his age. What he needed desperately was a deputy, preferably a young man who'd patrol the streets for him and had the speed of draw that would deter would-be felons from preying on the township.

Stevens had raised the matter often enough in meetings of the town council, but unfortunately Dos Santos was not a united community. Many of the council members were businessmen who depended for their existence on trading with saloon-owner Loyd Gubby. But if Gubby proposed a nomination for deputy marshal there were plenty of other folk who would suspect that he was putting forward a crony of his and would consequently vote against the motion. Another problem was the Irishman, Murphy who'd bought the rival North Star saloon under Loyd Gubby's nose a few months back. Murphy and his three rumbustious sons had quaint views on law and order that bordered on the anarchic.

The lawman was scratching his head helplessly under the accusing gaze of Pastor and Mary Stoller when Sheldon Darch and his two partners marched into the jailhouse. Stevens had been trying to explain to the young lady how dangerous it would be for one man to venture into the scene of an ambush.

When Darch informed him of their mission the relief showed in the town marshal's face.

'Would you like me to ride along?' he asked when he'd got over his initial surprise.

'Nope,' Darch replied coldly. 'Mr Gubby reckons you got plenty on your plate here in town. Me and the boys are taking a spare horse to bring the body in. If you like, you can warn the undertaker we'll be back after sundown.'

Mary Stoller stifled a gasp but then recovered her composure somewhat.

'Thank you, Mr Darch,' she said. 'And

please thank Mr Gubby too, and also Mr Lawson for raising the matter with Mr Gubby.'

The gunslinger turned and gave her a humorless smile.

'No need to thank Mr Lawson, miss,' he told her. 'Mr Lawson didn't do nothing, I'm the one who opened my big mouth....'

Over at the Mountain View saloon, lawyer Matt Lawson was sweating blood to convince Loyd Gubby that he'd worked wonders during his business trip to Denver.

'I spent your money on shares in two Denver banks, Loyd,' he explained. 'I also invested in railroad stock on your behalf, because the railroad offers the prospect of safe and generous long-term returns.'

He coughed as the saloon-owner blew a cloud of cigar smoke in his direction.

'Cut the horse-shit, Matt,' Loyd Gubby told him sharply. 'The reason I had that money to spend was because you let that crazy Irishman Murphy buy the North Star saloon right under our noses. It's here in

Dos Santos I need a solid base for my operations. Denver can come later.'

The lawyer didn't like being spoken to like that by a man ten years his junior. Unfortunately Loyd Gubby was no respecter of age or position. He was a coarse man by the lawyer's standards and dangerous when crossed. Lawson swallowed his pride and tried again.

'You already have a large interest in our local bank,' he pointed out patiently.

'If I'd got my hands on the North Star I'd own the two biggest saloons in Dos Santos,' Gubby grumbled. 'Then I could squeeze the smaller places into selling out; that way I could control the price and quality of all the liquor sold.'

'You hold the leases of many of the stores in our high street,' Lawson continued. 'And as for the North Star, Mr Murphy–'

'Murphy's an asshole,' Gubby said. 'Yet he managed to outwit us.'

'He's a friend of the North Star's former owner,' the lawyer explained. 'They did a deal over the sale. Nobody else even knew about it.'

'Hell, it's your business to know,' Gubby snapped. 'It's what you're paid for.'

Lawson lowered his gaze like a chastised schoolboy and fell silent. He knew that Murphy was no asshole; otherwise, he wouldn't be troubling Loyd Gubby. Murphy and his three sons were rough and tough and they kept their customers, miners and cowboys, in line with their fists and their boots.

'What's the position about the redskins?' the saloon-owner asked suddenly.

Matt Lawson's heart sank even further; the Indians were another running sore in their relationship.

'While I was in Denver,' he said, 'I checked out their rights of tenure to Poison Valley and the rest of the land they occupy.'

'What did you come up with?' Gubby demanded impatiently

'Everything's in order,' the lawyer said, and Gubby's face darkened still further.

'They could have moved west with the rest of the tribe ten years ago, but a few families decided to stay put. The army was too busy to worry about them at the time. Poison Valley was, and still is, worthless territory and uninhabitable. At the time there was no water on the rest of the ceded land either so an army major signed it over without giving it a thought. It's all recorded and legitimate; but Hank Morris has trading rights with the redskins, and you've bought into a partnership with Hank.'

'It's not trading rights I'm after, but land rights,' Gubby reminded him testily. 'I want to build a farm near that spring out at Eden Dale and those Indians are in my way.'

'Like I said, there was no water at the time of the agreement,' Matt Lawson said. 'The redskins reckon that their medicine man, Grey Wolf, conjured the spring out of the bare rock.'

The saloon-owner gave him a long, hard stare.

'Well, you'd better do some conjuring

yourself, Matt,' he told his visitor. 'I'm going to build that farm, Indians or no Indians.'

The cavalcade headed by Sheldon Darch was not the triumphant procession it was meant to be. Although word had spread through the main street about the attempted hold-up of the stage there was little interest in the gunslingers' mission. Loyd Gubby was not popular in Dos Santos, and neither were his hired guns; besides, there was no chance of bringing in the young cowboy alive, so why bother?

The only attention they attracted was when they rode past the rival North Star saloon. Two of the Murphy brothers were lounging outside and they made some uncomplimentary remarks about Darch and his partners in voices loud enough to be heard. The gunslingers had to bear the banter without riposte, since Gubby had warned them that he wanted no brawling with the unruly Irish family. But he had assured Darch that when the time came to settle the score, they would do it efficiently and with finality.

Corbett and Stiles were grateful for the rare opportunity to canter freely in the open countryside, especially now that the worst heat of the day had passed. It was an easy existence back at the saloon but it could also be long and tedious. Darch, on the other hand, was in a vile mood as they hit the trail; he'd spent most of the day in a boneshaker of a stagecoach and had foiled a hold-up almost single-handedly. Yet his only reward was to be forced to retrace his steps and seek out the remains of a worthless drunkard.

Occasionally his two companions exchanged sly grins and glances behind his back. Although they all worked for Loyd Gubby there was no love lost between them; Sheldon Darch was the boss's confidant and favourite and Corbett and Stiles were delighted to see that he was paying heavily for being so compliant with the saloon-owner's wishes.

The trail rose in a series of steps towards the mountains to the north. At last they reached a point from which they could perceive the pass ahead, though they were still miles away from it. Stiles took a look at the imposing crags through which the stage had travelled, and realized that their short holiday was over.

'If they're still up there in them rocks,' he observed to his two partners, 'we'll be foolish to venture too close. Just one feller with a decent aim will make short work of us.'

Corbett had already come to the same conclusion.

'A right jam you've got us into this time, Darch,' he grumbled. 'Why did you have to tell him about the stage? Were you boasting again?'

Sheldon Darch turned on him sharply.

'It weren't nothing to do with me,' he snapped. 'It's all down to that sonofabitch Lawson and that preacher feller. Lawson's sweet on the preacher's daughter, so when she started bleating about the feller we lost, Lawson ran straight in to tell Loyd Gubby and ask him to bring the feller's body in.'

At that moment Stiles interrupted their argument.

'There's someone moving up ahead,' he informed them. 'If he's come through the pass, them stage-robbers must have gone. If he's on his way there, they'll dry-gulch him and we'll know they're there.'

He smiled complacently at his own logic. After watching intently for a minute or so, he reached a conclusion.

'He's headed this way,' he told his companions.

'OK,' Darch said wearily. 'Let's check him out.'

As they drew closer to the rider they could see that he was slumped in the saddle, and that one side of his face was caked with blood. In fact, he looked a mess all over. Corbett turned in his saddle and glanced at Sheldon Darch.

'D'you know him?' he asked.

Darch nodded his head in disbelief; he couldn't believe his own eyes.

'I know him,' he affirmed. 'He's the feller the preacher sent us here to find.'

Stiles moved his right hand mockingly to his breast.

'Praise to the Lord,' he commented with a broad grin. 'Hallelujah!'

SEVEN

The next morning Billy Eason woke up with the sort of hangover he'd grown to expect over the last few months. However, this time some things were different. He opened his eyes and saw that he was in a small, tastefully decorated bedroom; for someone who was used to sleeping on bunks or even the bare earth, the mattress was soft and comfortable and the sheets smelt faintly of lavender.

He didn't have the usual feeling of guilt either. From what he could recall of the previous evening he'd been taken by his three rescuers to a kind of impromptu welcoming party at a local saloon. For some reason they all seemed grateful to him for what he'd done on the stage; he'd gone into the saloon without a cent in his pockets and he'd come out blind drunk again, all due to the generosity of well-wishers he'd never even met.

He raised his head and saw a clean shirt and pair of breeches laid neatly over the back of a chair. He stared at them and the old doubts returned. They weren't his. What had happened after the saloon? Had he broken into a place he had no right to be in?

There was a tap on the door and a small, trim, elderly lady came into the room.

'I'm heating a bath for you,' she informed him. 'If you're in anything like the condition your clothes were in when they brought you here, you'll be needing one.'

He tried to think of something to say, but his head was too sore. The woman went on in a firm, but not unfriendly tone.

'Mr Gubby sent those clothes over for you this morning when I told him that yours needed to go in the tub,' she said. 'I don't know if you're planning to stay; but if you do, I don't want you coming in in that sort of state again. Drinking I can tolerate in moderation, but I think the townsfolk could have found a better way of rewarding you for your bravery.'

His mouth was so dry that when he spoke the sound came out in a croak.

'I cain't stay here,' he told her. 'I ain't got no money.'

'Mr Gubby's seen to that,' the woman replied. 'Besides, you can always get a job, a young man like you.'

He went through the motions of bathing and getting into his new clothes in a daze. Then she served him strong black coffee, lots of the stuff, and he began to feel better.

'If you're wondering where your breakfast is, I haven't made you any,' the woman announced suddenly.

Breakfast was the last thing on the young cowpoke's mind, but she went on to explain none the less.

'The pastor has invited you to have lunch with him and his daughter,' she said. 'That's the young lady who's life you saved. Since they're expecting you at one, and it's almost noon already, I guessed you wouldn't be needing a breakfast.'

It was all starting to come together. His ignominious and accidental discharge of the shotgun and subsequent fall from the stagecoach had been taken as an act of bravery. It was all so ironic he'd have laughed if his head didn't ache so bad.

She began to clear the dishes away.

'By the way,' she said. 'My name's Rita Cole. What's yours?'

'Billy Eason,' he replied. 'I was born in Kansas. You make a mighty fine coffee, ma'am.'

'I ran a guest-house for most of my life,' she informed him. 'I gave it up a few years ago for health reasons. This time I'm doing it as a favour for the pastor. But I'm warning you, Mr Billy Eason, the same thing that I warned the pastor: you're only in my house on trial...'

When his landlady had given him clear directions how to find the pastor's house and church, Billy Eason ventured out into the sunshine. He had to find his way to the main street, walk almost its full length and then take a turning down towards the river.

On the way he passed several drinking-places, including the Mountain View saloon where he'd spent the previous evening. He'd have liked very much to go inside right now, but he didn't have a cent in his pocket and he'd probably exhausted all the hospitality Dos Santos had to offer.

As he walked he tried to picture in his mind the girl who'd been with him on the stagecoach. He'd actually only seen her for a brief time, but he recalled being struck by her golden hair and lovely features. He was glad that Rita Cole had insisted on his having a shave as well as a bath before setting out. Although he'd cut himself shaving in several places he looked better without a few days' stubble on his face. Even so, he'd still rather be heading for a saloon than for lunch with a pair of strangers.

A maid in her forties opened the door to him, and introduced him into a room where his hosts were waiting for him. As the girl rose from the settee to greet him she looked even lovelier than he remembered her, because now she was smiling whereas on the stage she'd seemed tense and ill at ease.

The preacher looked stern and solid, but he shook the young cowboy's hand warmly.

'I'm Pastor Stoller,' he said. 'I want to thank you for saving my daughter Mary's life.'

He was taken aback by their guest's reaction to his words; all the colour seemed to drain from Billy Eason's face.

'Are you all right?' the preacher asked. 'Perhaps you'd better sit down.'

'You haven't got over your fall,' Mary said, and the anxiety showed in her face. 'I'll get you a glass of water.'

The next hour was a torment for the cowboy. Both his hosts plied him with questions about his past life, while all he could think of was the way he'd messed everything up. So this was the Mary Stoller the hundred dollars were intended for, the hundred dollars he'd spent on debauchery. He ate very little and his hands shook as he raised the glass of water to his lips. Mary put it down to the effects of the accident, but her father had seen the signs before. It saddened him to think that such a pleasant young man was already in the grip of the demon drink, and he maintained a reserve towards Billy throughout the meal, whereas his daughter Mary was clearly blissfully happy in the young cowboy's company.

When lunch was over Billy was desperate to get out of the place, however beautiful Mary appeared to him. The girl sensed his unease and came to his rescue.

'I need a few things in town,' she told her father. 'Perhaps Billy would like to keep me company.'

Once outside in the open air, she was in no hurry to reach the stores. She'd misread the reason for his tenseness and she hastened to reassure him.

'Father can seem rather stern at times,' she said. 'I know that he likes you, but he won't betray his feelings.'

'He was fine with me,' Billy told her. 'You both were, and I'm grateful to you.'

'You must come again soon,' she said happily, but he didn't respond, so she decided to keep the conversation going on her own.

'I had an older brother,' she confided. 'When Ma died we were still quite young; well, I was very young because I don't really remember much about her at all. My brother Mark was years older than me, so he was much harder hit by her death. Pa tried to be both father and mother to us, but he was too strict for Mark's liking. In the end Mark rebelled and left home.'

Billy turned to face her. She was unbelievably lovely.

'Where's your brother now?' he asked, and her face clouded over.

'He's dead,' she replied. 'We didn't even know he'd enlisted, because he never wrote home. He was killed in one of the last skirmishes of the war – one that counted for nothing. My father changed after we got the news of Mark's death; nowadays he's much more tolerant of people's failings. But of course, it's too late and he realizes it.'

Billy just stood there, drinking in her beauty. He wondered when she'd get around to talking about Luke Mathews, and the thought tortured him. He could understand how Luke had fallen so deeply in love with this girl, and he despised himself for the way he'd let them both down. The only way he could stop himself getting involved was to get out of town. He was so deep in thought that he only just caught her next remark.

'I hope to see a lot of you while you're in Dos Santos, Billy.' She smiled.

'No, no,' he stammered, avoiding her gaze. 'I shan't be staying; I'm hoping to get work with the stage company.'

The girl couldn't conceal her disappointment. She reached out and took hold of his arm.

'Don't rush into anything, Billy,' she begged him. 'Loyd Gubby the saloon-owner was in our house this morning asking for my father's support. There's a meeting of the town council this afternoon, and Mr Gubby wants to get you elected deputy marshal of Dos Santos.'

It was almost sundown when the town marshal called at Rita Cole's house to meet her new lodger. When she showed him into the room, the cowboy was sitting on the bed looking pale and drawn. For a few moments Stevens just stood there looking him over; he'd heard so many conflicting stories about the young stranger who was the talk of Dos Santos, with some calling him a hero and others a pathetic drunkard.

Stevens had come bearing his own prejudices: it was Loyd Gubby who'd put up Eason's name for the job, and Gubby always put his own interests before those of the community. Only, the difference this time was that the saloon-owner's proposal had the blessing of the township's most respected citizen, Pastor Stoller. It was the preacher's support which had won over the neutral members of the council.

To his surprise Stevens's first impression of his new deputy was not unfavourable. The young fellow had a strong chin and an honest face, but then he noticed that Billy kept his hands clasped tightly in front of him. The marshal suspected that they'd be trembling if they were released.

'You got practically everybody's vote,' he informed the cowboy. 'You can start work tomorrow morning at eight. Since I sleep in the jailhouse you'll have to stay on here, or someplace else if this ain't to your liking.'

Billy nodded his head. He had mixed feelings about the offer. His instinct was to cut and run, but on the other hand a steady job might allow him to save towards the hundred dollars he owed Mary Stoller – if he could lay off the drinking, of course.

'You got any questions?' the lawman enquired, and the young cowboy shook his head. 'That's fine then,' Stevens commented as he turned to leave. 'The townsfolk gave you a vote of confidence today. Remember that you're working for the whole community, not just for Mr Loyd Gubby.'

At approximately the same time as Stevens was calling on his new deputy, lawyer Matt Lawson was visiting the Stollers' home on the outskirts of town. When the pastor's daughter heard the maid announce their visitor's name, she retired discreetly to her own room; Mary had had enough of the lawyer's company during the long coach trip from Denver.

Pastor Stoller listened in silence as Lawson came straight to the point. He wanted to warn the preacher that the young man he'd recommended to the town council needed to be watched carefully, since he had a bad drinking habit and a wild temperament. Stoller was intelligent enough to put two and two together: he'd been aware of the lawyer's infatuation with his daughter for several months, and here Lawson was, trying to destroy the reputation of the young stranger Mary had taken a fancy to.

When the lawyer had finished his diatribe, the preacher had a question of his own to ask.

'Tell me, Mr Lawson,' he said in an even tone. 'Did you vote against Mr Eason in the meeting this afternoon?'

His visitor blushed bright scarlet and mumbled a response in the negative.

'Well, I guess that makes the two of us about equal in responsibility,' Stoller remarked. 'But thank you for your concern.'

But later, when the lawyer had left, Pastor Stoller thought deeply about the matter. Mary, his daughter, meant the world to him and he hoped that she wasn't heading for misery.

Billy Eason was still trying to get to sleep when he heard the tap on his window. He reached for his gunbelt and slid his Colt from its holster before going to investigate. When he opened the window an arm thrust a bottle towards him from out of the darkness.

'It's for you,' a voice said. 'Leave your window open from now on, in case you're out when I call.'

EIGHT

The way Beatrice Lawson saw it, the business excursion to Denver had done her husband no good at all. The lawyer was preoccupied and withdrawn throughout the following week and, as usual, he refused to disclose the root cause of his worries. When she tried to approach him on the matter he brushed her irritably aside.

'It's business matters, Beatrice,' he snapped. 'You just see to the house and let me worry about the rest.'

But the house was empty and soulless; they had no children, though Beatrice was now in her early thirties, some ten years younger than Matt. Fortunately, he never reproached her on the subject though she knew that he adored children and would have wanted a family of his own.

As consolation the lawyer buried himself in his work and in the harmless pursuit of other women – harmless because he always seemed to be chasing some impossible dream and, as far as his wife knew, none of his intended lovers had ever responded favourably to his advances.

For weeks now she'd been waiting for the chance to sit him down and talk things over with him, but first there was the trip to Denver that got in the way, and now he obviously wasn't in the mood to listen to anything she had to say. Then, at the start of the new week he came home smiling and more relaxed, as if he'd suddenly seen a light in the tunnel.

'I'd like to invite some friends over for lunch next Sunday,' he announced. 'Would that be possible?'

'Of course, Matt,' she assured him, then took a deep breath before asking: 'Who are they, Matt?'

'Well, there's Loyd Gubby for a start. I'd also like to ask Sandra Drake from the

Double D spread and her young brother Ricky.'

The surprise showed on his wife's face. She'd been expecting Mary Stoller's name to crop up among the proposed guests. What had happened to her? Had she been replaced so early in the lawyer's affections? Sandra Drake was a beautiful young woman too, but she rarely ventured into town and Matt Lawson hardly knew her.

Lawson could almost read his wife's mind as she digested his statement. She was starting to suspect that something was up again, so he hastened to reassure her.

'I want to introduce Loyd to the Drakes,' he told her. 'He's looking for some place suitable to build a house outside of town. His mind is set on taking a piece of the redskins' land and I don't think that's wise, nor even legal if it comes to that. The Drakes have got land to spare; I'm hoping I can work out a deal between them over a good meal.'

Beatrice looked happier now. Why

couldn't her husband always come clean like that, like in the old days? Her own news could wait, at least until she was certain of her facts. She turned her mind to more practical considerations.

'The Double D is a couple of hours' ride away,' she pointed out. 'Are you sure that Sandra and Ricky will want to come?'

'I've thought about that too, Beatrice.' He smiled. 'That's why I chose a Sunday, because that's the day the ranchers come to church.'

The lunch went better than Beatrice Lawson had anticipated. She was feeling rather nervous because she didn't entertain very often, and the Drakes were more or less strangers to her. Loyd Gubby she knew better, but didn't like; Gubby was unpopular in Dos Santos and some of that unpopularity had rubbed off on to her husband, since the two men worked closely together.

After they'd got over their initial shyness the Drakes turned out to be open and friendly. They were both brown-haired and brown-eyed; Sandra, whom she guessed to be about nineteen years of age, had her hair cut short but that didn't detract a bit from her natural beauty. Her brother Ricky was no more than sixteen but he already had the good looks and ready smile that Beatrice suspected would soon wreak havoc among the young ladies of the territory.

In the course of their conversation Sandra and Ricky explained that they had been orphaned several years previously; their parents had both been drowned while trying to negotiate a river in flood on their way back to the ranch from town. Fortunately, the experienced ranch foreman, Ed Smith, was also an old friend of the family. With the help of two cowhands he'd kept the spread going, and now Ricky was old enough to help as well, as his muscular frame and suntanned skin testified.

Loyd Gubby had no time for small talk and he was glad when Beatrice Lawson had finished questioning her young guests.

Gubby wanted to get down to business, which was why they'd all been invited here in the first place. To Matt Lawson's dismay the saloon-owner ignored all the advice he'd been given about the possible purchase of a tract of Double D land.

Instead, Gubby launched into a long invective against the Indian families occupying the area to the west of the Drakes's spread. If he thought that his words were going to impress the young brother and sister, he was very wide of the mark.

'We get on well with the Indians, the little we see of them,' Sandra Drake informed him. 'If our cattle stray on to their land Grey Wolf sends someone over to let us know so that we can round them up again. That only happens occasionally in the dry season when some of the streams run dry.'

'It don't seem right to me that redskins have got water when white folks' cattle go thirsty,' the saloon-owner commented.

The irritation showed in his voice; he wasn't used to being contradicted. Ricky

Drake hastened to back his sister up.

'We never run out of water altogether,' he said. 'It's just that the cattle head for what's nearest, and sometimes that takes them on to Grey Wolf's land.'

'Tell me what's gonna happen when you want to expand?' Gubby asked suddenly.

'Expand?' Sandra asked. 'Why should we want to expand? We're fine as we are.'

Gubby bit the end of a fat cigar and lit it lovingly before replying.

'Every business has got to expand,' he told her. 'Nothing can stay the same for ever. If a thing stays the same it dies, and that goes for ranching, the same as for banking or saloon-keeping.'

Loyd Gubby had got round to one of his pet theories, but Beatrice Lawson was more interested in studying her husband's face as the debate progressed. She was pleased to note that he was paying no more attention to Sandra Drake than to their other guests. In fact, Matt was looking rather at a loss as to the direction the discussion was taking.

Then, with female sensitivity she observed a subtle change in Loyd Gubby's attitude. From being argumentative and confrontational he became amiable and reasonable, tolerant of the young ranchers' opinions.

There were only two explanations, Beatrice concluded: either the saloon-owner was concealing his true feelings; or maybe he was falling under the spell of the lovely young girl sitting opposite him.

That same Sunday Rowly Harris set out as usual for the Indian settlement in the hills. It was the first Sunday of the month, the day designated by his boss, storekeeper Hank Morris, to take supplies of food and clothing to Grey Wolf and the other redskins in accordance with the agreement reached some years earlier between the tribe and the army. Morris ran a successful general store on the main street of Dos Santos, and his business was enhanced still further by his license to supply and trade with the Red Indians.

The wagon the old-timer was driving was piled high with the goods his employer was authorized to sell. But underneath the pile, wrapped carefully in old blankets, lay a store of hard liquor that Morris sold to the younger members of the tribe – a trade that was quite illegal, and frowned on by the military authorities.

However, the army had long since lost interest in the region now that it was more or less pacified. They had plenty of trouble on their hands much further north in Sioux and Cheyenne country, while many miles to the south the border with Mexico was always a potential trouble spot.

Grey Wolf, the small tribe's medicine man and leader, knew very well what was going on behind his back, but the esteem he'd once enjoyed throughout his community had been eroded by the humiliations the Indians had had to endure over the years. Now his wise counsel could only influence those who were prepared to listen to him, and sadly some of the younger braves would not.

At the half-way point in the journey the trail crossed a pleasant rivulet that was always fordable even in mid-winter and only dried up when the drought was really severe. It was here that Rowly Harris stopped to water the horses, roll himself a smoke in the shade of the wagon and close his eyes for twenty minutes or so.

On this occasion, his reverie was disturbed by the arrival of two horsemen who approached the wagon from out of the sun. To his consternation he saw that their faces were obscured by neckerchiefs. As they rode up one of them drew a gun and kept him covered, though the only weapon the old-timer had, an old carbine, was lying uselessly on the seat of the wagon.

Rowly was in no position to protest as the other rider got up on the wagon and began to rummage about. Anything breakable he threw violently to the ground, and he seemed to take particular pleasure in smashing the store of liquor bottles to smithereens.

'Save a couple to drink on the way back,'

the man who'd drawn his gun told his companion. 'Even if it is only Gubby's piss-water.'

When the carnage was over the two masked men turned their attention to the old-timer, who hadn't said a word throughout the proceedings.

'It's a shame it ain't Darch or one of the others,' one of the men said. 'But let's pistol whip the sonofabitch anyways.'

When Rowly Harris finally found his way back to Dos Santos and the sanctuary of the Mountain View saloon he was in pretty bad shape. All he could remember about his two assailants was that they both spoke with an Irish accent.

NINE

Loyd Gubby was so incensed by the news of the destruction of the Indian consignment that Matt Lawson had his work cut out dissuading the saloon-owner from taking immediate revenge.

'If you send Darch and the boys over to the North Star,' he pointed out, 'the Murphys will be waiting for them. They'll cut them down, and they'll have the law on their side.'

'The law!' Gubby exploded. 'What's Stevens got to do with it?'

'Plenty,' the lawyer retorted. 'It's his problem from start to finish. Hank has a legal commitment to those redskins, and it's up to Stevens to provide an escort if the stuff isn't getting through.'

Gubby started to cool down and think

more clearly. The town marshal wouldn't want to go himself so he'd have to designate his new deputy. Gubby had kept Billy Eason in drink for over a week and so far he'd had no return on his investment. Matt was right; if Stevens sent Eason and the drunk got gunned down by the Murphys, the Irish sons of bitches would lose the support of the townsfolk. That would be the time for Darch and his partners to make their move.

It was Hank Morris the storekeeper who approached the marshal for protection. Although Stevens guessed that Loyd Gubby was behind it, it was a request that he couldn't reasonably refuse.

'OK, Hank,' he agreed without enthusiasm. 'Next trip you make, Billy Eason will ride along as well.'

In a way Stevens was pleased to put his young deputy to the test. So far, Billy had made no mistakes, though it was obvious to the old lawman that he was still drinking. Stevens couldn't figure out where the youngster was getting the stuff, since he'd had no reports of Billy drinking in any of the town's saloons. But the stench of alcohol was on his breath each morning when he reported for duty, and by the end of the day he always seemed jittery and anxious to get back to his lodgings.

Another puzzle to the marshal was the relationship between his deputy and Mary Stoller, the preacher's daughter. Mary was too sensible a girl to provoke gossip by calling on Billy at the jailhouse, but she never missed an opportunity to bump into him casually and exchange a few words when he was on his rounds in Dos Santos. Stevens could read young people well enough to know that Billy reciprocated the young lady's feelings, but for some reason his deputy held back and seemed almost troubled by her attentions.

By mid-week Hank Morris had assembled another consignment for the Red Indian settlement. This time, however, there was a difference. Because the law was riding along as well there was no liquor concealed under the merchandise.

The ride out was trouble-free, but Hank Morris seemed nervy because of the previous trouble.

'If anyone comes too close,' he told the young deputy sitting alongside him, 'shoot first and ask questions later. That goes for them redskin varmints, too. When you get to know them as well as I do, you'll see they're a bunch of liars and thieves. They should have been driven west like the rest of the tribe. And don't you listen to any stories about their medicine man, Grey Wolf – about him making magic and curing sickness and all that hoss-shit. He's a liar and a thief like the rest of them.'

As he spoke, the storekeeper glanced across at his passenger. Billy looked pale and tense. Hank had heard about the deputy's drink problem and it didn't fill him with confidence. All in all, he breathed a deep sigh of relief when the tepees and shanty dwellings came into sight.

'That's Grey Wolf's wigwam,' he indicated with a nod of the head. 'That's him lounging outside with them filthy squaws of his.'

Billy turned his head and saw that the wigwam was just like all the rest. If Grey Wolf was indeed the leader of the small tribe, there was no ostentation in his lifestyle. Two women were sitting on blankets at the entrance to the tepee, engaged in some sort of weaving or embroidery work. Grey Wolf himself sat a few yards away from there, his eyes closed as if he were asleep or meditating.

'I do my trading in that clearing over there,' Hank Morris informed the deputy marshal, pointing to a space among the wigwams some hundred yards further on. 'You'd better stay here. They ain't used to strangers, and that badge of yours may set them off.'

Billy wondered if the storekeeper might have other reasons for wanting him out of the way, but he raised no objection; he'd been sent to protect Morris, not to investigate his business dealings. The wagon trundled off to where a crowd of Indian braves were already assembling.

Billy stood there and gazed at the seated medicine man. The Indian's tanned and lined features reflected an inner calm that the youngster envied. He found it hard to guess at the man's age; his body was as lithe as a thirty-year-old, but the wisdom of his expression belonged to a much older man.

Suddenly Grey Wolf's lips moved almost imperceptibly, just loud enough for the nearest squaw to hear. She laid down her handiwork and got to her feet. She went into the tepee and emerged again holding an earthenware cup. She brought it over to Billy Eason and he saw that it contained clear water. He drank it gratefully and handed it back with a few words of thanks. Then it occurred to him that Grey Wolf hadn't opened his eyes to know that someone had got off the wagon.

Only a few moments later the young deputy

was jolted from his reverie by the sound of raised voices from over where the trading was taking place. It looked as if things were taking an ugly turn, but still there was no change in the tribal leader's expression. Billy decided to go and see for himself. Hank Morris seemed almost marooned on the seat of the wagon, surrounded by a throng of young braves, none of them more than sixteen or seventeen years of age. Fortunately, their discontent was vocal rather than physical for the moment at least, and they allowed Billy to push his way through to where the wagon stood.

'Get up here, Billy,' Hank Morris shouted. 'Use your gun if you need to.'

The deputy obeyed the first command but he had no intention of drawing his gun in the middle of a hostile settlement. From what he could gather, the young braves were demanding the quota of firewater they'd become accustomed to.

'Lying varmints,' Hank Morris snarled, his face red with anger and embarrassment.

'They ain't never had liquor from my store.'

To Billy's dismay, the storekeeper picked up the rawhide whip and made as if to lash out at the bystanders. It was a crazy action and Billy knew he had to stop him, otherwise they'd be torn to pieces. As he tried to wrestle the whip away, both of them tumbled from the wagon on to the hard earth. Billy landed on top of Hank, and jumped to his feet immediately. The storekeeper wasn't so lucky; he stayed sitting on the ground, clutching his left arm.

'You goddamned sonofabitch,' he sobbed, his face racked with pain. 'You've gone and broken my arm!'

Meanwhile, above their heads, the young braves had begun looting the wagon...

Town Marshal Stevens scratched his head in disbelief as his young deputy related the story to him.

'But you say that nothing was stolen,' he commented. 'You got everything back from the redskins?'

'That's right,' Billy assured him. 'Grey Wolf saw to that. When he raised his voice they all went quiet as lambs.'

'I hate to think what Loyd Gubby's gonna say about it,' the marshal said. 'He got you this job, he's paid for your lodgings and even for your horse to be stabled. You do know that Gubby's got an interest in Hank Morris's store, don't you?'

Billy shook his head sadly; he knew nothing about the saloon-keeper, who seemed to own half of Dos Santos. All he did know was that he needed to repay his debt to Gubby as quickly as possible.

When the deputy got back to Rita Cole's place he was a bundle of nerves. After picking at his evening meal he retired to his room and stretched out on the bed. He closed his eyes but was too depressed to sleep.

It was dark when he heard the tap on the window. He got up and opened it; the bottle of rye whiskey had been left there as usual. As he reached for it, the window frame was pulled down again with force. He stifled a scream as a sharp pain shot up his arm. Then the window was open again and strong arms were dragging his upper body out of the room. Someone grabbed his hair to stop him resisting, and punches rained on to his head and face. Eventually he took a vicious one on the point of the jaw, and slipped into oblivion.

By the time the news had reached the Stollers' house, all of Dos Santos had heard of the cowardly attack on the deputy marshal. Mary Stoller rushed over to the boarding-house in a panic, but fortunately Rita Cole was at hand to allay her fears.

'Doc Daly has given him a thorough examination,' she informed her anxious young visitor. 'He couldn't find any fractures, but it was a vicious attack and Billy is going to take a little while to get over it. Yes, you can see him if you like, but don't stay too long, as he's very tired.'

Billy Eason opened his eyes when she came into the bedroom and instinctively turned his face away. He didn't want her to see him looking like this, didn't want to distress her in any way. There was a chair by the wall and she sat down without saying a word.

Only the sounds of the township were audible, but he could detect the faint fragrance of the girl's perfume as he lay there. Suddenly he felt a wave of calmness envelop him, the kind of calmness he'd observed with envy in Grey Wolf's face. He realized with regret that this feeling would not last. When Mary Stoller departed he'd be left with his usual problems.

Many minutes must have passed before the landlady called to her visitor from the passageway.

'I'm coming, Mrs Cole,' Mary replied, and Billy turned his head towards her for the first time, only to see a tear trickling down her cheek. Mary rose from the chair and came over to the bed. She lowered her head and kissed Billy very tenderly on his swollen lips, and it felt as if she was applying a balm to them.

'I'll call again,' she promised him. 'And I'll pray for you to get well – *really* well.'

TEN

When the shot echoed around the walls of the canyon it took Luke Mathews, and his horse, completely by surprise. It must have been a very near miss, because the animal bucked suddenly and threw its rider violently to the ground.

Luke lay there stunned for a few moments, but then his agile mind began to work overtime: the nearest cover was over twenty yards away, and since he didn't know from which direction the bullet had come, he couldn't be sure he was safe even if he reached the boulders. More than likely, he'd be nailed as he tried to get to his feet.

He decided to grit his teeth and stay where he was. Luckily his right hand had ended up a few inches from his holster. If the shooting started up again he'd have to do something;

125

in the meantime it was wiser to play possum and await developments.

The minutes ticked by like hours as he lay there. His horse came over and nuzzled against his ribs for a few seconds, then moved away again, leaving him to feel even more exposed.

He heard stones sliding some distance away. His assailant was coming out of hiding. He prayed silently that he wouldn't hear any conversation; if there was more than one of them he was doomed. But still the only sound he heard was of gravel being crushed underfoot, a sound that was coming ever nearer. Then someone spoke.

'Steady there, my beauty,' the voice said. 'I don't want you coming to any harm, do I?'

It sounded calm and unruffled, and very familiar. His attacker had obviously been taken in by his ploy. Luke opened his eyes and saw that the man had taken hold of the horse's reins. Luke swivelled his body and drew his Colt from its holster.

'Hi, Danny,' he said, and the youngster

froze visibly for a moment.

He should have stayed that way, but instead he tried to turn, clawing frantically for his six-shooter as he did so. Luke Mathews sent a slug crashing into his chest from about ten feet and Danny Richards staggered backwards before sinking to his knees, spewing blood on to the brown earth.

Luke lost no time in getting out of the canyon the way he'd entered it. He didn't know where Marvin Richards was, but he had no desire to meet up with his old army buddy ever again. He had no idea if Marv was behind the dry-gulching or even knew of his brother's intentions. What was certain was that Marv would come looking for his young sibling, and when he found him he'd have only one thought on his mind: revenge.

He rode straight back to Laramie and visited several saloons, making sure to mention in each of them that he was heading west.

'I aim to reach the coast before the bad weather sets in,' he informed his acquaintances. 'I hear there's good times to be had in San Francisco.'

Although he did head westward at first, his plan was to make his way south in a series of loops that would throw any pursuer off the scent. He realized now that he should have listened to Billy Eason in the first place. All of a sudden he'd lost his zest for the wandering life. The township of Dos Santos seemed to be calling him from afar, urging him to come home.

It took him weeks to wind his way through the hills and mountains until eventually he emerged on to the Colorado plains far to the south. For days he rode past landmarks that had once been familiar to him. His journey brought him eventually to a pleasant ranch in the lower hills. A roughly-hewn sign bore the name of the spread, the Double D.

As he rode past the corral a middle-aged man came out of one of the barns and stood there watching him. Luke rode up to him and raised his hand in a greeting.

'Hi,' he said. 'Do the Drakes still own this place?'

'That depends,' the cowpoke replied enigmatically. 'Which Drakes are you talking about?'

'Mr and Mrs Drake who had the place ten years ago,' Luke replied. 'They always brought their kids into Dos Santos on Sunday mornings.'

'They drowned,' the man informed him. 'It's the kids who own the place now, only they've grown up some. I'm Ed Smith, the ranch foreman. Cain't say I know you, son.'

'I been away for a long time, but now I'm back; at least for the time being. My name's Luke, and I'm pleased to meet you.'

He was thinking quickly. He couldn't very well set up as a gambler in his home town. What he needed was an honest job and a place to stay.

'You wouldn't have any work here, would you, Mr Smith?' he asked.

The ranch foreman eyed him up and down rather sceptically

'You don't look much like a cowboy to me, son,' he remarked.

'You're right,' Luke admitted with an open smile. 'But I've done many things and I ain't never starved...'

Sandra Drake looked up from her paperwork when Ed Smith came into the room. She had a lot on her mind. Ever since the meal at the Lawson's place, saloon-keeper Loyd Gubby had been sending her flowers via one of his gunslingers and trying to get her to go to Dos Santos and visit him. His attentions were unwelcome, but she knew that he was too powerful a man to offend.

'What is it, Ed?' she asked.

'There's a young feller outside asking about work. He used to live in town but he's been away for years.'

The girl frowned; could this be some trick Loyd Gubby was playing on her?

'Where is he?' she asked without committing herself.

'Outside in the yard,' Smith replied.

She crossed to the window and peeked out. When she saw the stranger her heart missed a beat; his face had matured and bore the lines of experience but she recognized him at once. He had once been the mischievous youth she remembered from her visits to church with her parents in happier days. She'd never forgotten the crush she'd had on him then. Now he was back and fate had brought him straight to the ranch. As she stood there watching him, she suddenly had the feeling that her life might never be the same again.

ELEVEN

When Mary Stoller discovered that Billy Eason had left town she was devastated. A visit to his lodgings having proved fruitless, she decided to try the jail house, only to hear the bad news from Marshal Stevens himself.

'All I know is that he's gone off to be by himself for a while,' the lawman told her. 'When I offered him his wages he only accepted a couple of dollars. He told me to give the rest to Rita Cole or Loyd Gubby. He said that if he still owes them, he'll pay the rest later.'

'So, he's coming back then,' Mary said hopefully.

'I don't know,' the town marshal replied. 'By my reckoning he didn't look fit enough to be travelling, but he got his horse from the stable and rode off.'

Grey Wolf didn't seem at all surprised to see the young deputy ride up to the Indian settlement and dismount in front of the medicine man's tepee. His visitor came straight to the point.

'I need your help,' he said tersely, and Grey Wolf led him inside the wigwam so that they could talk in private.

In a matter of minutes Billy blurted out all his drink problems and how they affected his ability to think straight and act honorably. After his confession he enquired whether the Indian could offer him any hope of a cure.

'I can take you where you may get help,' Grey Wolf told him. 'It lies beyond Poison Valley; it is the place where my ancestors made their medicine, but I cannot promise that it will work for you. Do you need to return to Dos Santos?'

'Nope,' Billy assured him, though he felt a pang of regret for the way he'd walked out on Mary Stoller without a word of explanation. 'I have all the time in the world.'

The medicine man looked very grave, as if he didn't relish the task he was undertaking.

'We'll set out for Poison Valley at once,' he said. 'Have you brought firewater with you?'

Billy had to steel himself to tell the truth.

'Yeah,' he admitted. 'I spent my last couple of dollars on the stuff. I need it for the moment.'

'You are right,' Grey Wolf agreed. 'But you will have to make it last. We shall be away many days.'

As they rode, the medicine man spoke to his young companion about what he knew of the situation in the township of Dos Santos.

'The man they call Gubby is an enemy of the Indians,' he said. 'If he becomes more powerful he will make much trouble for us and drive us from our land. The town marshal is a good man. When you first came, I could see that you, too, are a good man. You must go back and help Marshal

Stevens; he needs men like you.'

When night fell they set up camp deep in the depression known as Poison Valley. Grey Wolf explained that there were water holes in the valley, but that most of them were alkaline, and very few contained fresh water. Travellers desperate with thirst had often been lured by the sight of water, only to find that it was undrinkable, and some of them had never made it to safety.

Before bedding down for the night Billy Eason drank about a third of a bottle of whiskey to make sure he'd get to sleep. To his surprise, his companion made no comment, no criticism. No sooner had the redskin stretched out on the ground than he was snoring peacefully, whereas the young deputy marshal had to await the effect of the alcohol before he was able to drift into sleep.

The following morning, as soon as Billy stirred under his blanket, Grey Wolf was crouching at his side.

'What do you want?' he asked the white

man. 'Whiskey or water?'

Billy was hardly awake, but the taste of the previous night's drink was still in his mouth.

'Whiskey,' he said, and then gulped the liquid the Indian handed him.

As he lay there, he heard the sound of the horses moving away and he turned his head to see what was going on. Grey Wolf was riding off, with Billy's horse in tow. The deputy threw the blanket to one side and struggled to his feet.

'Hey!' he yelled. 'Where are you going with my horse?'

Grey Wolf swivelled round in the saddle.

'I'm going to water them,' he replied. 'You must start walking towards those hills, so that I know where you are. I shall be back at noon.'

It took a few moments for the implications to sink into the young cowboy's fuddled brain.

'You come back here,' he ordered. 'I'll ride with you.'

But Grey Wolf rode on unconcerned, and

Billy's hand dropped to his holster. It was empty, and now he was powerless to stop the redskin's departure.

That moment was the start of a nightmare that was to last for many days. Each time Grey Wolf reappeared he offered his companion the choice of the whiskey or the water. It was a hideous decision to have to make; he craved both at the same time, and suffered, whichever choice he made. For days he was feverish, and when he chose the whiskey as an immediate relief for his suffering he always became even more dehydrated and sick.

And all the time Grey Wolf kept a respectful distance, so that all Billy's plotting to surprise him and overcome him were to no avail. He cursed his tormentor both out loud and mentally; never had he hated anyone with so much venom. At other times he resorted to pleading, but the medicine man was in no mood to show him pity.

As the days passed, logic began to prevail

again, and Billy realized that water was always the best choice to make, though the craving for alcohol still racked his body. He began to reason with the Indian, pointing out that all this torture was useless, since he would eventually find himself in a saloon one day and begin hitting the bottle again.

'Or do you want me to die out here in these goddamned hills?' he enquired. 'Is that the reason you're doing it?'

Grey Wolf didn't answer him, but he could see that the wildness had left the youngster's eyes. At last he was making progress.

Then, one day, Billy failed to make it to the appointed rendezvous. The medicine man caught up with him hours later at one of the holes that held drinking-water. Billy had left the beaten track and had got lucky.

'You made me afraid,' Grey Wolf told him. 'I thought you would die of thirst. Why were you so foolish?'

Billy was sitting calmly by the side of the water hole. He'd washed the stale sweat off his face and body and was looking much better. He felt better, too – better than he'd done for many moons.

'I wasn't foolish,' he replied. 'I just got sick of depending on you, like I got sick of depending on whiskey to be able to go to sleep at night and get up again in the morning. Anyway, I knew you'd come looking for me.'

Grey Wolf studied his face for a while before riding up to the water hole and dismounting. He reached into a saddle-bag and handed Billy his Colt .45.

'Here you are,' the Indian said. 'It is your chance to kill me as you have been threatening.'

Billy sheathed the gun in the grim knowledge that a week or so earlier he'd have used it on his companion.

'You can pour the rest of the whiskey away,' he told the medicine man.

'No,' Grey Wolf said. 'You get rid of it.'

Billy walked up to his horse, plunged his hand into one of the saddle-bags and took out a full bottle of whiskey. With the medicine man looking on he uncorked the bottle and raised it to his lips. He filled his mouth with the hot liquid, then spat all of it out on to the ground.

When he'd emptied all the bottles and left a dark stain on the dusty trail he turned to face Grey Wolf.

'You know something?' he confessed. 'Even when I lived for the stuff, I never did like the taste!'

TWELVE

When Marv Richards found his brother Danny's body on the floor of the canyon his grief was soon followed by the desire for revenge. At the same time he cursed his own stupidity in letting his younger brother talk him into the hare-brained scheme to dry-gulch the gambler.

'I know you don't want to be the one who guns him down, Marv,' Danny had said. 'Like you said, he saved your life once; but me, I never did like the smart sonofabitch, and we sure could use some of that bankroll he was flashing last night in Laramie. You head on to Cheyenne like you said. I'll join you when I'm finished here.'

But Danny had never shown up, and Marv Richards had been forced to retrace his steps. By the time he'd found his brother,

141

Danny wasn't a pretty sight. All Marv could do was to cover the corpse with stones to prevent further damage from scavenging animals and birds.

He'd racked his brain trying to recall the conversations they'd had when they were together in the army. He knew that Luke hailed from somewhere in Colorado Territory, and he vaguely remembered him talking of a place called Los Santos, or something along those lines. Of course, Luke might not return there, but he might still have relatives there, or folk he was fond of. In that case, even if he couldn't get even with Luke in person, he might be able to get at him through someone close to him. And then Marv remembered that Luke had spoken of a young girl...

Sheldon Darch was standing near the window of the Mountain View saloon, idly watching the townsfolk pass by in the afternoon sunshine. Then a horseman came into sight at the far end of the main street and rode slowly past the stores and hotels until deciding to stop outside Loyd Gubby's establishment.

Darch studied the stranger's face through the saloon window; it was a long, horsey sort of face with lines carved deep by the weather and experience, but not by excessive age. It wasn't the most intelligent face Darch had seen, and now, as the rider sat in the saddle staring at the board bearing the name of the saloon, the gunslinger wondered with a little smile if the stranger had difficulty reading it.

Whatever it was that had attracted his attention, the horseman dismounted, tethered his mare and entered the bar-room of the saloon. He ordered a cold beer and took a couple of sips before addressing the bartender again.

'The L. Gubby whose name is writ on the board above the window, would that be Loyd Gubby, maybe?'

The bartender glanced across at Sheldon Darch, but the gunslinger's face was expressionless. The only other people in the room were Corbett and Stiles, who were playing a friendly game of euchre in a far corner. When the stranger asked the question they both laid their cards face down on the table and turned to eye him up and down.

Although the newcomer was an unknown quantity, the bartender felt he had sufficient backing from the three gunslingers to counter with a question of his own.

'Why should that be of any interest to you, mister?' he enquired bluntly.

Marv Richards could read the situation without having to have it spelt out to him. The bartender wouldn't answer like that unless he had friends in the room.

'Nothing,' he replied with no trace of irritation in his voice. 'Forget that I asked.'

Darch turned and glanced towards the two card-players. Stiles got the message and rose from his seat. He sauntered casually across the room to the door of Loyd Gubby's office and, for once, went in without knocking.

The saloon-owner was sitting behind his desk, deep in thought. He was not a happy man: his arch-enemies, the Murphys from the North Star, had made a fool of him by raiding the supply-wagon he owned jointly with storekeeper Hank Morris and destroying the concealed liquor it carried; the deputy marshal he thought he had in his pocket had decided to bite the hand that fed him, and had since high-tailed it out of town after the beating Corbett and Stiles had given him; and the Drake girl from the Double D ranch was showing no sign of responding to Gubby's advances. Worse still, rumour had it that Sandra had fallen for a penniless drifter who'd turned up at the ranch looking for work.

And then there was the medicine man Grey Wolf and his redskin scum, who occupied the land Gubby coveted. And what was his lawyer, Matt Lawson, doing about it? Nothing. For days now Lawson had seemed to be walking about in a dream that even the saloon-owner's ill-temper couldn't wake him from.

When Stiles burst into the room uninvited, Loyd Gubby knew that it was for something important. In his present mood, Gubby expected it to be yet more bad news.

'What is it, Stiles?' he snapped. If it wasn't important he'd make the gunslinger pay for his impudence.

'There's a stranger at the bar asking questions about you,' Stiles told him, 'like as if he knows you from somewhere. Darch thought you'd better be told.'

Gubby got up and walked over to the wall. He slid a metal cover to one side to reveal a peep-hole through which he could survey most of the saloon. He had to wait a few moments until the stranger turned his head to one side to reveal the profile of his face.

'Well, I'll be damned,' Loyd Gubby exclaimed as he recognized the newcomer.

'If it ain't that sonofabitch Marv Richards.'

The shouting could be heard clearly in the North Star saloon, some hundred yards away. Before long the story had reached the ears of the Murphys: there had been a row between a stranger in town and Loyd Gubby's hired guns. The stranger had been evicted from the Mountain View saloon and was now drinking his way towards the Irishmen's establishment.

Marv Richards looked the worse for wear when he eventually staggered into the North Star. As the proprietor, Jack Murphy, served Richards a cold beer his three sons, Phil, Mick and Pat were eager to know what grudge the newcomer had against their rivals.

'Loyd owes me five hundred dollars from way back,' Richards informed them. 'He wouldn't pay up right away. He reckoned I should go back there at sundown and then he'd pay me – maybe. That's when we started rowing.'

'How comes he owes you all that money?' Pat, the youngest Murphy, enquired. 'What did you do for him.'

Richards turned and eyed him balefully.

147

'That's between me and Loyd,' he said sharply. 'What's it got to do with you, boy?'

The brothers felt their hackles rise at his remark. They weren't used to being talked to like that. But their desire to score over their old enemy Loyd Gubby made them bite their tongues.

'We don't want to know your business, mister,' Phil Murphy assured him. 'Only we don't want to see you cheated out of what you're owed, neither. Say, Pa, what if us boys go over to the Mountain View with our friend here? If Gubby welshes on him we can sure blacken his name in Dos Santos.'

It didn't take their father long to give his consent.

'Go you,' he told them. 'But no trouble, right?'

'Why don't you come along too, Pa?' his son Mick suggested. 'You're gonna miss the fun.'

Jack Murphy would have loved to go, but recently he'd been experiencing chest pains and breathlessness, though he hadn't breathed a word of it to his sons.

'I got enough to do here,' the old man replied. 'You can tell me all about it when you get back.'

The youngest brother Pat was disappointed by the lack of interest their grand entrance caused in the Mountain View saloon. Pat had not been allowed to take part in the hold-up of Hank Morris's wagon, and now he was hoping for some excitement to make up for his exclusion.

As it was, Sheldon Darch didn't even glance up from his newspaper when they burst through the swing-doors. Phil Murphy looked around the room and saw that Corbett was cradling a glass of whiskey at the far end of the counter, while Stiles was standing quietly near the window, scratching his armpit. Any ill will the hired guns felt towards Marv Richards was certainly well concealed.

Phil led the entourage over to the bar and ordered a round of beers. As the bartender was pouring the drinks, Mick Murphy fixed him with a challenging stare, but the man merely ignored him and set the glasses down without uttering a word. The saloon was fuller than on Marv Richards's previous visit; the clientele consisted mainly of middle-aged townsfolk who were settling down for an evening game of dice or cards.

Suddenly, Marv Richards addressed the bartender in a loud voice.

'Go tell Loyd Gubby that his old friend Marv Richards wants to see him,' he said, and Pat Murphy sniggered by his side.

As he spoke, the office door near the foot of the stairs opened wide and the saloon-owner emerged from his lair. At the sight of him, Marv Richards detached himself from his companions and moved along the bar. Then, unexpectedly, Richards drew his gun and Mick Murphy felt his heart give a lurch. He glanced round at his elder brother, but Phil was just standing there like a statue.

Behind them, unnoticed, Corbett had also drawn his Colt. He raised it and fired two slugs into Phil Murphy's back. Mick spun round to meet the threat, clawing for his six-shooter as he moved. Sheldon Darch fired through the pages of his newspaper and brought Mick to his knees with a single shot. Corbett then finished the job with a bullet angled downwards between his shoulder blades.

Meanwhile, the youngest of the Murphys was in headlong flight for the swing-doors. As he reached them, Stiles closed in on him like a snake. His slug shattered Pat Murphy's cheekbone and he went down screaming and spitting blood. Stiles watched his agony with fascination for a moment or two, then at a sharp command from Sheldon Darch he finished the youngster off with a bullet through the chest.

Some of the customers had sought the safety of the floor when the shooting began; others had seen it all and were just sitting there, the shock visible on their faces. They watched Loyd Gubby and the stranger amble over to the bar together.

'Let's have a beer, Marv,' Gubby said amicably, 'while we're waiting for the law to show up.'

THIRTEEN

Lawyer Matt Lawson's untypical detachment from the wheelings and dealings of the business community of Dos Santos could be traced back to the bombshell that his wife Beatrice had dropped at the breakfast table a few days earlier.

Lawson was nibbling at a piece of toasted bread and studying the morning gazette when Beatrice announced suddenly:

'I'm pregnant, Matt. I'm going to have a baby.'

She waited almost fearfully for his reaction. Their marriage had been rocky for several years, and she suspected that it was only Matt's concern to avoid gossip that had kept them together. His undisguised admiration for some of the younger females in the township amounted almost to mental cruelty. Would her pregnancy be good news to him, or merely another shackle on his freedom?

He put the paper down and stared at her across the table.

'If this is your idea of a joke, Beatrice,' he said coldly, 'it's in bad taste.'

'It isn't a joke, Matt,' she replied. 'I was fairly sure weeks before you went to Denver. Now I can feel the fluttering inside me. Doctor Daly is sure, too.'

Her husband took a deep breath and rose from the table.

'I've left some papers upstairs,' he said vaguely. 'I'll go get them.'

When he reached the bedroom he went in and closed the door behind him. He could feel small tears starting to run down his cheeks, and instinctively he fell on his knees at the side of the bed and thanked God for the blessing He'd bestowed on the household.

When he came down again he was smiling as she hadn't seen him smile in years. He went straight over to her and embraced her warmly.

'Do everything the doc tells you, my darling,' he told her. 'And if you need me for anything you must tell me, even if I'm in the middle of work...'

When news of the shooting at the Mountain View saloon reached the lawyer's office his heart sank. What mischief had Darch and the other gunslingers been up to this time? He'd rather have kept away, but Loyd Gubby was his principal client and might need him. He thought of his baby, as yet unborn, and prayed that all Gubby's ambitions would be achieved quickly so that Dos Santos could enjoy a period of peace and prosperity.

Marshal Stevens had beaten him to it, but the puzzlement on the lawman's face indicated how little he understood of the causes of the killings.

'Me and Loyd was brought up together,' a long-faced stranger was telling the town marshal. 'When I rode into town and saw his name on the saloon I thought I'd pay him a visit. I ain't had much luck lately and my brother was gunned down a few weeks back. Loyd was glad to see me; he said that I should come back at sundown and he'd have some money for me to help me out.'

Several of the men standing listening in the bar-room knew that the stranger had been thrown out of the saloon earlier in the day; but none of them dared say a word, not with Darch and his two *compadres* looking on.

'When I talked about it in the North Star saloon a bit later on,' Marv Richards continued, 'three Irish fellers bought me drinks and said they'd come along with me to Loyd's place. I saw no harm in it, not till I saw one of them go for his gun when Loyd came out of his office to meet me. And that's when the trouble started.'

Marshal Stevens glanced around the room at the customers who'd also witnessed the action.

'Have any of you got anything to add?' he asked.

'Only that the floor can do with a good clean,' one joker remarked. 'That's where I dived when I heard the first shot!'

The lawman didn't feel like laughing.

'I don't know how Jack Murphy's gonna take this,' he muttered to nobody in particular.

In fact, over at the North Star saloon Jack Murphy had taken the news of his sons' massacre badly – very badly. In his rush to get across to the rival establishment he'd collapsed in agony and had had to be carried upstairs to his bed. Later that night the word spread that the Irishman had suffered a massive heart attack and was fighting for his life. The next day one or two of Jack's friends began boarding up the windows of the saloon. The North Star was closed until further notice.

Despite Matt Lawson's appeals for restraint Loyd Gubby was on the crest of a wave after the elimination of his arch-enemies the Murphys. He couldn't wait to resolve the problem of the Indian settlement, which was a constant thorn in his side. How long could those red devils hold on to their land and prevent its development and exploitation by entrepreneurs such as himself?'

The first casualty of the saloon-owner's ambition was a young Indian brave called Broken Wing. The youngster was returning from a hunting expedition in the hills when he noticed that his pony was heading straight for a couple of white riders coming from the opposite direction.

Broken Wing was no lover of the white race, since the older men in the tribe had filled his head with stories of the atrocities done to the indigenous natives by the cruel greed of the invaders from the East. However, he had no quarrel with the cowhands of the Double D ranch, whose territory he was now skirting. Grey Wolf, the medicine man, had established a rapport with the young brother and sister who ran the spread, and redskins and cowboys always exchanged greetings when they met on the trail. He hoped that the horsemen coming in his direction worked for the Drakes too.

They didn't, but at least he knew one of them quite well; it was the old-timer Rowly Harris, who drove the trading wagon for the Dos Santos storekeeper Hank Morris. The other rider had a hard glint in his eye, and looked a man to be wary of. Whereas Harris raised his hand in greeting, his companion merely spat in the dust as the Indian brave passed by. Broken Wing ignored the insult, but he could feel his old hatred for the white men well up inside him.

Rowly Harris was annoyed by Sheldon Darch's attitude; after all, Darch didn't earn his living by going among the Indians and trading with them. The old-timer didn't understand why Hank Morris, on Gubby's orders, had told him to ride alongside the unsociable gunslinger in the first place. He'd lost the habit of riding on horseback, and his buttocks were raw and sore from the saddle.

Darch reined in suddenly and wheeled his horse around. Harris followed suit and saw that the gunslinger was watching the young Indian's back as the pony ambled on in a leisurely manner. Then Darch drew his rifle from its scabbard and raised it to his shoulder.

For a moment the old-timer thought that Darch was just fooling round, but then the rifle cracked and the Indian brave slumped in the saddle briefly before sliding sideways on to the hard ground.

The gunslinger looked very satisfied as he replaced the rifle in its case.

'Let's go check that he's dead,' he told his shocked companion. 'Then we'll use his knife to slaughter a couple of calves.'

FOURTEEN

After he'd filled the water-troughs in the yard and the corral, foreman Ed Smith ambled over to the wood-barn where the new cowhand was chopping logs for the ranch-house fire.

In the short time he'd known him, Smith had come to like and respect the new recruit. Everything about Luke Mathews, his smart clothes and his unscarred hands, indicated that he'd been used to easier ways of making a living than cowpunching. Yet he'd knuckled down to his new life without complaint, and seemed eager to learn under the guidance of the experienced Ed Smith.

Luke's arrival at the spread had allowed Ricky Drake more time to spend on the range, which was where he loved to be. And Sandra Drake didn't seem to be missing her brother's company all that much. She couldn't disguise her liking for the handsome newcomer, and she always found excuses to bump into him around the ranch house or call on him to do some small task for her in the course of each day.

What Ed Smith liked most about Luke was that he hadn't let the mistress's favours go to his head. If she asked him to do anything, he always checked with the foreman that it was all right for him to leave what he was doing and attend to the young lady's wishes. Smith learned quickly that Luke's temperament was by nature boisterous and mischievous, but Luke showed nothing but respect for his two employers, though they were both his juniors in age. When one of the older cow-pokes made a harmless joke about Sandra Drake's unconcealed liking for him, Luke would reply amiably: 'She's young; when she gets to know me, she'll soon change her mind!'

The ranch foreman didn't think so; Luke might be easy-going, but he had a sharp mind, and nobody pushed the jokes too far. Behind the amiability, Smith suspected, there lurked a steel-like strength of character and also the ability to back it up with action. Smith had watched Sandra Drake grow into womanhood and he wished her nothing but happiness; the way he saw it, if she was going to settle down with a feller, she could do a lot worse than Luke Mathews.

'Another few logs should do it,' he told the young cowhand, who'd worked up quite a sweat. 'When you've finished, go get yourself a drink of water from the well.'

As he spoke he heard horses approaching. He walked back to the doorway and was surprised to see Loyd Gubby and Sheldon Darch ride into the yard. Gubby was looking very serious; when he saw the foreman standing in the doorway he said:

'Are the Drakes about?'

'Miss Drake is in the house,' Ed Smith informed him. 'Her brother's not here.'

As the two horsemen made for the ranch house, Sheldon Darch turned suddenly in the saddle.

'Do you spend much time on the range?' he asked the foreman.

'Whenever I can,' Smith replied. 'Why d'you ask?'

'Because,' Darch said with a leer, 'there's lots going on out there you don't seem to know about.'

Luke Mathews left his wood-cutting and came out and stood at the foreman's side. When the two visitors dismounted in front of the house, Gubby muttered a command to his companion before going in through the open door. Darch dutifully remained outside and rolled a smoke while he waited.

Sandra Drake looked up from the pastry she was mixing and had a feeling of unease when she saw the saloon-owner standing watching her. Loyd Gubby glanced around the room and was disappointed to see none of his flowers on show. Sandra invariably consigned every bunch to the compost heap as soon as she received them, so that they couldn't remind her of her unwanted admirer. She was surprised by his visit, and even more surprised by what he said.

'The redskins have been slaughtering your cattle,' he told her. 'My man Darch and Rowly Harris caught two of them cutting up some calves they'd killed. Darch managed to kill one of them as he tried to run off. Rowly knows the Indians pretty well and he recognized the one who got away: it was Grey Wolf, their so-called medicine man.'

The astonishment showed in the girl's face.

'But, why?' she said. 'Grey Wolf has always been our friend.'

'It's in their nature,' Gubby said sanctimoniously. 'They've probably been living off you for years.'

No, she thought, Ed Smith would never have missed something like that. And why should she take the word of a hired gun rather than Grey Wolf, whom she'd known and liked for years?

The look of perplexity on her young face made her even more alluring and desirable to the saloon-owner. He was a man who was used to getting what he wanted, and at the moment Sandra Drake was what he wanted most in the world.

'That's Loyd Gubby going into the ranch house,' the foreman informed his companion. 'He's the one who's been sending Sandra them flowers she don't want. The feller guarding the door is Sheldon Darch, Gubby's top gun.'

Luke Mathews wasn't happy about the visitors, but he didn't see what he could do about it. Fortunately, Ed Smith was full of ideas.

'Take the logs over to the house,' he told the younger man. 'And don't forget your gunbelt.'

Luke didn't need to be told twice. He buckled his belt and picked up an armful of firewood. He wasn't unduly worried about Darch's reputation; Luke was starting to feel the benefits of healthy living on the ranch, and he felt sharper even than when he'd relied on quick reactions during his gambling days.

Ed Smith watched like a hawk as Luke crossed the yard to the front door of the ranch house. At the last moment, Sheldon Darch moved to intercept him.

'The lady has a visitor,' the gunslinger said, with a tight, mocking smile. 'Leave the wood here, or come back later.'

As he finished speaking, Luke heard Sandra's voice raised inside the house; she sounded angry and distressed. Luke immediately unburdened himself of the logs, which landed heavily on Darch's feet and ankles. The gunslinger's face registered pain and surprise for an instant, before Luke's left hook landed on the side of his jaw and stretched him out on the dust. Meanwhile, the ranch foreman was moving as fast as the weight of his shotgun allowed.

'Go on in, Luke,' he ordered. 'I've got this one covered.'

Loyd Gubby spun round to face the newcomer. The saloon-owner's shirt front was white with flour from Sandra's attempts to push him away. Gubby was angry that Darch had let the upstart get past him, and his hand dropped instinctively to the butt of his Colt .45. The next moment he was staring at the barrel of Luke's six-gun.

'I think you'd better leave, mister,' Luke advised him. 'You've overstayed your welcome.'

The two visitors left in utter humiliation, since Sheldon Darch was almost too groggy to keep upright in the saddle. When they'd vanished from sight, Ed Smith turned to Luke and said:

'You be careful from now on, son. You've just made yourself two dangerous enemies.'

'Thanks for the warning,' Luke replied. 'But I can look after myself; you've no need to worry about me.'

'It ain't you I'm worried about, but Sandra Drake,' the foreman told him. 'I just don't know what she'll do if something happens to you.'

When Loyd Gubby and Sheldon Darch got back to Dos Santos there was more bad news awaiting them. Billy Eason had returned to the township and had been reinstated as deputy by the marshal.

Eason had recounted his experiences in detail to the lawman, and naturally the medicine man Grey Wolf featured prominently in his story. Grey Wolf and he had been constant companions during the latter part of Eason's absence from Dos Santos and there was no way the Indian could have been sighted on Double D land. Confronted by Marshal Stevens with the new evidence, Rowly Harris was forced to concede that he might have been mistaken in his earlier identification.

'What about the rest of your story?' the lawman demanded. 'Are you sticking by that?'

Rowly nodded his head, but didn't dare meet the marshal's gaze. Stevens didn't believe him, and neither did most of the town's citizens. The next day Rowly didn't report for duty at Hank Morris's store on the main street. He'd ridden out of town during the night, accompanied by another horseman whose identity was obscured by the darkness. Whatever fate befell him, Rowly Harris never showed his face in Dos Santos again.

FIFTEEN

Pastor Stoller could tell from his daughter's jittery behaviour that Billy Eason was back in circulation. For a while he hesitated about what advice to give her, if any at all. The preacher had never forgiven himself for the strictness that had caused his son to leave home so young and lay down his life in the war. Eventually, however, he felt he had to speak his mind.

'If it's Billy you're fretting about, Mary,' he told her one evening, 'don't go rushing over to welcome him back. I like him, but he's got a lot of problems that only he seems to know about. Maybe they're so many that nobody can help him solve them.' When his daughter made no response, he added lamely: 'I just don't want you to get hurt, that's all.'

Sandra Drake was horrified when Ed Smith told her he'd given Luke Mathews the day off to ride into town.

'How could you?' she rebuked him. 'You know how powerful Loyd Gubby is in Dos Santos.'

'That's just what I told him,' the ranch foreman replied. 'But he said he had business in town and it wouldn't wait. It was too early to wake you. Besides, you've always told me that I'm in charge of the cowhands.'

Sandra's young brother Ricky was standing there, listening to them.

'If you like, I'll go in after him,' he suggested, but Sandra shook her head vehemently.

'You keep away from Dos Santos, Ricky,' she said sharply. 'I'm worried enough as it is. I hope Luke hasn't gone there looking for trouble.'

'I don't think he's that stupid,' Ed Smith said. 'I'm sure he'll keep his wits about him.'

Even as he spoke, miles away in Dos Santos, Marv Richards was gazing idly out of the front window of Loyd Gubby's Mountain View saloon, when he spotted the familiar figure of his old comrade-in-arms Luke riding casually up the main street.

Although Billy Eason felt more in control of his actions than he had for many moons, the youngster was still beset by worries: there was the money he owed Mary Stoller for a start, and also the news of Luke's death, which he'd kept from her for his own personal reasons.

Mary was constantly on his mind; if only he'd known her years ago, as Luke had. Unlike Luke, he'd never have left her behind to go adventuring. When the preacher's daughter didn't come to see him after his return to town, he felt a contrasting mixture of relief and longing to see her. Had Mary forgotten him so quickly?

It was about eleven o'clock one bright morning that he saw her again. She was crossing the street some thirty yards along from the jailhouse, where the deputy marshal was on solitary duty. She'd been shopping; and was probably on her way home, her blonde tresses dancing in the sunlight.

As the girl neared the bank, a man emerged from its doorway and Billy Eason gave a gasp as if he'd seen a ghost. The man was the spitting image of Luke Mathews, whose dead body he'd left behind in the canyon outside Laramie. Billy squinted his eyes to make sure; there must be some mistake, but there wasn't. It was Luke Mathews, large as life and smiling as if he was very glad to be home.

Billy moved quickly to the doorway and out on to the street. By now, Mary Stoller had seen Luke as well. After a moment's hesitation she dropped her parcels on the ground and ran into the gambler's welcoming embrace.

Now that he was over the initial shock of seeing his old friend resurrected from the dead, Billy's spirits sank as he saw the couple cling to each other with such affection. The experience was so painful to him that he was forced to avert his gaze. That was when he noticed the elder of the Richards brothers, Marvin, standing in a shaded section of the sidewalk nearby.

A myriad of questions raced through the deputy marshal's mind. If the Richards brothers had travelled south with Luke, who'd fired the shots in the canyon, or had it all been merely another of Luke Mathews's tricks? If Luke had come back to reclaim his lost lover, what would he do when he discovered that Billy had squandered the money intended for her?

Then he saw Marv Richards's hand drop on to the butt of his revolver, and an even more ominous thought came to him. What if Marv Richards wasn't with Luke, but was stalking him? When he saw Richards slide the gun from its holster Billy knew he had to react quickly.

As the first shot rang out Luke Mathews

dragged Mary Stoller down on to the ground and tried to cover her with his body. Passers-by ran for cover as Billy's answering shot shattered the window immediately behind where Marv Richards was lurking.

Cursing his first, poor shot, Richards swivelled round to face the new challenge. He and the deputy marshal fired simultaneously, but in turning Richards had spoilt his aim, and his slug embedded itself harmlessly in the wall of the jailhouse. The gunslinger winced with pain as Billy's shot took a chunk of flesh out of his thigh. Billy was closing in now, both arms outstretched to steady the heavy .45 Colt. Richards raised his gun, but in vain; Billy's next shot smashed into his chest, high up, and threw him backwards on to the planks of the sidewalk. By the time the deputy reached him, Marvin's eyes were staring lifelessly up at the blue sky.

Billy walked slowly back to where Luke Mathews was helping Mary Stoller to her feet. Both men were still wary, and Billy in particular had reason to suspect their problems weren't over.

'That's Marv Richards lying over there,' he said. 'His brother may be with him.'

'His brother's dead,' Luke replied. 'I killed him the day you and me split company. That's why Marv came gunning for me.'

Mary didn't understand all this talk of killing, but she did know that she was indebted to the young deputy marshal.

'You walked out without a word, Billy,' she said. 'And now you're back, and you've just saved my brother Mark's life!'

Later that afternoon, at the Stollers' home, the prodigal son was happy to relate his adventures to a captive audience, comprising his father, his sister and the friend who'd just saved his life.

'My outfit was caught up in Sherman's advance to the coast in the last few weeks of the war,' he explained. 'A handful of us got separated from the main body and tried to take shelter in a farmhouse. Before we

177

reached it a shell burst nearby. I was the only survivor and I was badly shaken up. I hid in a barn that night. Next day I found that I'd spent the night in the company of a corpse, a farmhand who'd been shot through the head. My uniform was a problem to me; I didn't want to be gunned down or sent to some army prison, so I switched clothes and started the long hike westwards.'

'But Billy knows you as Luke Mathews,' Mary said. 'When did you change your name?'

'I never could forgive Ma and Pa for naming me after three of them Evangelists,' Luke explained, with a rueful grin in his father's direction. 'Matthew Mark Luke Stoller. I never did like Mark, which was the name my folks called me by, so when I enlisted I told everyone to call me Luke. Later, when I was on the run from the Yankees, I just turned my name around so that I couldn't be traced and rounded up.'

'I went into the canyon to look for you,'

Billy said, hoping to ease at least part of his sense of guilt. 'You weren't moving. I was sure you were dead.'

'That's what Danny Richards thought, too,' Luke grinned. 'It was his last mistake.'

'But now you're back,' his sister said happily. 'You've come back home.'

'Well, as far as the Double D ranch at least,' Luke replied. 'After years of gambling and thinking how smart I was, I guess I've found something I really enjoy doing, though I've still got plenty of learning to do. I can promise Pa one thing, though: all my fancy tricks are a thing of the past.'

The old man was listening with tears in his eyes. God had brought his son home to him from the dead; and, reformed or not, Luke would always be his son.

Then it was Billy Eason's turn to relate, or rather to confess, his misadventures to the whole family. The only thing he could be proud of was his hard-fought victory over alcohol, and even that was down to the efforts of the medicine man Grey Wolf. The hardest part was recounting how he'd squandered all the money Luke had given him, including the hundred dollars meant for Mary Stoller. Typically, his partner was quite unconcerned.

'Earlier today I decided to follow the advice you once gave me, Mr Deputy Marshal,' he said. 'I've put all my savings into the local bank. You just make sure the bank don't ever get raided, and we'll call it quits!'

SIXTEEN

Lawyer Matt Lawson sat behind his desk and listened to the two redskins with growing unease. If they were telling the truth a crisis was looming that could ignite the whole territory. And the evidence was there in front of him, a small pile of gold-dust and nuggets that Laughing Dog and Little Cloud had brought with them.

'It comes out of the ground with the water,' Laughing Dog explained. 'And when the water dries up it is covered by the dust.'

Lawson took a deep breath.

'And you're sure the place is on Indian land?' he enquired.

'It is deep within Poison Valley,' Little Cloud confirmed. 'It is owned by our race on the word of your Great White Chief.'

Lawson doubted if the President had

heard of Colorado Territory, let alone Poison Valley, but the redskin was right about the treaty.

'What does your medicine man Grey Wolf have to say about this?' he asked.

'He does not know about it,' Laughing Dog replied. 'Only a few of us hunt in the valley, as did our fathers before us and their fathers, too. Grey Wolf thinks like the Indians of long ago: everything belongs to the tribe. Now the white man rules and we must think like him. This gold belongs to me and Little Cloud, but we come to you for help because we are told you are wise in such things.'

After the Indians had left, having obtained a promise from the lawyer that he would start proceedings for their claim, Lawson agonized for almost an hour about what he should do. Eventually, his fear of Loyd Gubby overcame all his scruples. If he acted without informing the saloon-owner, he knew he was a dead man and his child would be born fatherless. He decided to go over to the Mountain View saloon at once and get the whole business off his chest.

Loyd Gubby's reaction to the news was typically vigorous. There was no way that a gold strike so close to Dos Santos was going to escape his grasp. Matt Lawson tried to urge caution, but to no avail.

'Who ever heard of redskins mining for gold?' Gubby exploded. 'We gotta settle this right away.'

Within the hour he had it all organized. He'd send two of his hired guns out to Poison Valley to find out exactly what was going on. Lawson would have to go as well, and also Hank Morris who ran the general store in partnership with Gubby himself.

'But I can't go,' the lawyer protested. 'Beatrice isn't having an easy pregnancy. And Hank Morris still has his arm strapped up.'

The saloon-owner's eyes narrowed with displeasure.

'You'll both do what you're told,' he snapped. 'Hank will have to see the land for himself to decide what sort of tools will be needed for us to make a quick start. And you'll need to survey the strike before you start drawing up any legal documents. We cain't afford any mistakes. Besides, you ain't going to be in any danger; my men will see off any savages that bother you.'

Sheldon Darch was not surprised to learn that Corbett and Stiles had been chosen for the mission. Loyd Gubby had been cool with him ever since the débâcle out at the Double D ranch house. Darch had the feeling that Gubby would happily dispense with his services if someone better turned up. For a short while Marv Richards had seemed destined to fulfil that role, but the deputy marshal's quick thinking had scotched that.

Meanwhile, Darch had been doing some thinking of his own. He'd already become less distant with the other two gunslingers, since one day they might all end up in the same boat. From now on Sheldon Darch was determined to put his own interests first.

The small party of riders set out at daybreak the following morning. Beatrice Lawson stirred and smiled when her husband planted a delicate kiss on her cheek before departing. He'd become so attentive and affectionate towards her, it was like a second honeymoon. But this kiss meant more to the lawyer than any other, because Lawson had a premonition that the mission was ill-fated.

They rode all day and watered the horses on the few occasions that they stumbled upon a residue of drinking water in the scorched earth. All the time, Hank Morris complained about the pain in his arm and the discomfort the long ride was causing him. When at last they halted and prepared a scratch meal, Corbett announced that Hank and Matt Lawson would share the watch throughout the night.

'But that ain't fair,' Morris objected. 'You and Stiles are years younger than Matt and me.'

Stiles gave an ironic chuckle.

'You been telling us all day that you ain't gonna sleep because of the pain in your arm,' he pointed out. 'If you're gonna be awake, you may as well keep watch. Me and Corbett will need our wits about us tomorrow. When them redskins realize what we're up to, they're gonna get pretty sore.'

Lawson didn't get involved; all his thoughts were on his wife back in Dos Santos. When Hank Morris grudgingly agreed to take the first watch, the lawyer was the first of the group to spread his blanket and settle down for the night.

When Lawson awoke, the first rays of dawn were visible on the eastern horizon. He rubbed his eyes and wondered why the storekeeper had let him sleep that long. The answer was simple: Hank was stretched out on the ground a few yards away, snoring softly and obviously oblivious to any pain.

Lawson threw the blanket to one side and got to his feet. There was something wrong. Although the horses had been hobbled, only two of them remained at the camp. He looked around in vain for the other two horses and then aroused the sleeping gun-slingers.

When Stiles realized what had happened he went over to where Hank Morris was lying and kicked his bandaged arm savagely. The storekeeper screamed with pain, but nobody felt much sympathy for him.

'You lazy sonofabitch,' Stiles yelled. 'You've let them red varmints get away with two of the horses. What are we gonna do now?'

It was Corbett who answered him.

'We'd better make tracks right away,' he said. 'The closer I get to Dos Santos the better I'll feel.'

Matt Lawson decided that only he had the status to take command in the present situation.

'We'll have to ride two up,' he stated. 'If the horses show signs of tiring, we'll have to take turns walking.'

Stiles turned and leered at him.

'You two sons of bitches were supposed to be keeping watch, mister,' he snarled. 'I ain't killing no horse to save your fat ass. You'll both wait here till we get help.'

Despite his aches and pains, Hank Morris could still think clearly and he wasn't buying any of Stiles's arguments. They'd die out in the wilderness before help could arrive, and he didn't fancy being found and tortured by the redskins either. Stealthily, he began reaching for the gun hidden under his blanket.

Corbett was watching his every movement; the gunslinger walked nonchalantly behind him and drew his Colt smoothly. He thrust the barrel between Hank's shoulder blades and fired a single shot that severed the storekeeper's spinal cord.

Matt Lawson just stood there, dazed by the nightmare he was living through. As the two gunslingers began seeing to the horses, he wondered how long it take one of them to realize that he was a witness to callous murder. He started walking away from them, unobserved, and then broke into a run. He'd gone over fifty yards before he was brought down by a fusillade of shots.

'Shall we go see if he's dead?' Corbett asked his companion, but Stiles shook his head.

'Leave him,' Stiles said. 'I'm told the savages like scalping folk who are still alive.'

When the two gunslingers made it back to the Mountain View saloon, they found that Loyd Gubby had gone out to a business meeting. They poured their story out to Sheldon Darch, who assessed the situation swiftly and shrewdly.

'You cain't tell Gubby you killed his two closest associates,' he told them.

'But it weren't our fault, Darch,' Stiles replied. 'What else can we tell him?'

'What he'll want to hear,' Darch said with a sly smile. 'Tell him that the Indians jumped you to steal the horses. Lawson and Hank got killed in the fight, that's all.'

And that was the story they did give the saloon-owner, and it spread quickly around the town. Feelings against the redskin settlement were running pretty high and there was no shortage of volunteers to form a posse and ride out to Poison Valley.

But when the marshal and his companions reached the scene of the crime late the next day they found only the corpse of Hank Morris where Corbett and Stiles had left him. Lawyer Matt Lawson's body had mysteriously disappeared!

SEVENTEEN

Ricky Drake was the first to spot the cortège of redskins approaching the ranch house. Foreman Ed Smith had gone out on the range, leaving Ricky and Luke to look after the ranch. Smith wanted to see for himself how their calves had been slaughtered, and to try to ascertain who was responsible for the crime.

When the Indians halted in the yard in front of the house, Luke went out of the barn to back up his young employer in case there was trouble. He saw that one of the horses was dragging a litter with a white man lying on it. In the meantime, Sandra Drake had appeared at the front door of the ranch house to greet Grey Wolf, who was at the head of the small band of redskins.

The medicine man's ruse about the

goldstrike had worked; he'd lured his enemies into a trap and almost destroyed them as an organization. But there was no triumph in his voice as he spoke, since Loyd Gubby was still alive and scheming in Dos Santos.

'We have brought you the lawyer Mr Lawson,' he told the girl. 'He is very sick, but I think he will live. I have helped him all I can, but now he needs white man's medicine. We have brought two horses we found there as well.'

Ricky and Luke converged on the stretcher. Matt Lawson's face was deathly pale, but he summoned up all his strength to speak.

'Loyd Gubby's men did this,' he said, his eyes bright with fever. 'Corbett and Stiles. They killed Hank. Tell the marshal – I want justice!'

When the buckboard drove slowly through town driven by Luke, with Sandra Drake in the back tending the stricken lawyer, the word spread like wildfire that Lawson had survived the Indian attack in Poison Valley. As soon as they'd delivered the wounded man into the hands of Doc Daly, Luke and Sandra proceeded at once to the jailhouse to report to the marshal.

Both Stevens and his deputy Billy Eason were at the jail to hear the story. When Luke had finished speaking, the town marshal shook his head slowly.

'If Lawson hadn't survived to tell us the truth,' he commented, 'I'd have gone ahead and called the army in; then we'd have had an Indian war on our hands.'

There was a knock on the door and Billy went and opened it. The visitor was Mary Stoller, Luke's sister.

'I came as soon as I heard,' she told them. 'People are saying that Matt Lawson isn't dead.'

She glanced nervously across at Sandra Drake; the two young women shared the fear that something momentous was going to happen, and that their loved ones were going to be sucked into it. It was Luke who broke the silence.

'I'm going over to Loyd Gubby's place,' he announced. 'I've had a long ride and I could do with a drink.'

He pronounced the saloon-owner's name with a certain degree of venom, as he recalled how Gubby had attempted to force his advances on Sandra Drake. Marshal Stevens detected Luke's suppressed anger, and wanted to harness it for the good of the township.

'Let me swear you in as a deputy, Luke,' he suggested. 'I need good men to help me clean out Gubby's nest of vipers.'

'You can count on me, Marshal,' Luke replied. 'But I ain't gonna wear no badge. I'll walk into Gubby's saloon like any other customer.'

Before Sandra could stop him, he'd opened the door of the jailhouse and walked out into the sunshine. Billy Eason turned to the marshal and said:

'I'll give him a couple of minutes; then I'm going after him.'

He was careful to avoid eye contact with either of the young women who were standing there so anxiously.

'I'll go with you,' Stevens said. 'This is my responsibility.'

Billy Eason shook his head.

'I'll go alone, Marshal,' he said. 'I've worked the saloons with Luke; we can read one another's minds. I'd rather you stayed here. If anything goes wrong you can pick up the pieces.'

Over at the Mountain View saloon Sheldon Darch and his fellow gunslingers could sense the changed atmosphere in the township. Beatrice Lawson had rushed over to the doctor's to be close to her husband. Business associates of the stricken lawyer had called there as well, and the truth about the shootings in Poison Valley was soon common knowledge among the citizens of Dos Santos.

There were more customers than usual drifting into Gubby's saloon, and they were whispering among themselves and casting meaningful glances in the direction of

Gubby's hired guns. The saloon-owner himself was upstairs in his living-quarters, blissfully unaware of the gathering storm clouds. He was looking through some personal documents he kept in his solid iron wallsafe, which he also used to keep ready cash for use in the bar-room downstairs.

Sheldon Darch could read the unease on the faces of Stiles and Corbett. Neither man had really relaxed since Matt Lawson's body had gone missing from the scene of their crime. Darch had urged them to stay calm and await developments, but now even he could feel the tension in the air as if a trap was closing around them.

Then, when Darch saw his old enemy from the Double D ranch walk nonchalantly through the swing-doors of the saloon, he sensed that matters were about to come to a head. But Luke didn't even spare Darch a glance as he sat down at one of the few vacant tables in the bar and proceeded to deal himself a hand of patience.

Corbett and Stiles were standing at

opposite ends of the counter. Darch made for the wide staircase without haste. As he passed where Corbett was stationed he muttered a warning in a low voice.

'Keep an eye on the feller who just came in,' he said. 'He's full of tricks.'

Corbett placed a restraining hand on his arm.

'What's going on, Darch?' he demanded. 'Where are you going?'

'Upstairs to see Gubby,' Darch told him with a hint of irritation in his voice. 'You just keep an eye on the stranger. Don't let him get the drop on you.'

He proceeded on his way up the stairs, half-expecting Luke to call him back, but the gambler-turned-cowhand merely concentrated on his silent game of cards, as if the room was deserted.

Darch had only just gone out of sight when the doors of the saloon swung open again and Billy Eason walked in, wearing his badge of office on his shirt front. The room fell silent and every head turned to watch him make his way to the counter and ask for a glass of cold water to slake his thirst.

Corbett glanced at Stiles and the latter nodded his head imperceptibly. Stiles was only a few yards from where Billy stood sipping his drink; if the deputy gave any trouble, it would be Stiles who would deal with him. Meanwhile, the nervous types among the customers were starting to make their way stealthily to doors leading to the street outside.

Loyd Gubby was deep in thought when he heard someone knock at the door of his living-quarters. He couldn't understand why the town marshal hadn't taken measures already to rid the territory of the red vermin who'd murdered Matt Lawson and Hank Morris. The disappearance of the lawyer's body was a puzzle, of course, but surely the rotting corpse of Hank Morris was reason enough to call the army in. Gubby couldn't help wishing that the Indians had scalped Morris while they were at it, if that was what was needed to stir

Stevens into action.

'Who's there?' he enquired, closing the document he'd been perusing absent-mindedly.

'Sheldon. We need to talk. It's important.'

Gubby went over to the door and unlocked it, then returned to his leather armchair. Darch closed the door behind him before he spoke.

'They've brought Matt Lawson in,' he said. 'They've taken him over to the doc's house, so he must still be alive.'

The saloon-owner had been cool towards the gunslinger of late, but now he smiled warmly at the news.

'That's great, Darch,' he commented. 'Now the marshal will have to do something about them redskins.'

'He'll do something, all right,' Darch commented laconically. 'That's what's worrying me.'

Gubby had struck a match to light a fat cigar, but now the flame hovered in mid-air.

'What do you mean?' he asked.

'It was your own men who gunned Lawson and Morris down,' Darch informed him. 'The Indians had taken two of the horses. Morris wanted to make sure of a ride home, and Lawson backed him up. Corbett and Stiles killed them; they had no choice. The only pity is that Lawson lived to tell the tale.'

The saloon-owner's disbelief soon turned to rage.

'When did you know this?' he demanded.

'When they got back,' Darch replied. 'They were going to tell you the truth, but I told them to blame the redskins, because I knew that's what you'd want to hear.'

'You lying sonofabitch,' Gubby exploded. 'You've lost us everything. You're finished in this town.'

'We all are, Loyd,' Sheldon Darch reminded him. 'Lawson's got too much on us – and especially on you.'

Gubby wiped the sweat from his forehead. If his men had levelled with him earlier he'd have had time to formulate a plan. The news had been sprung on him too late.

'What are we going to do, Sheldon?' he asked.

'You're on your own, Loyd,' the gunslinger said coldly. 'I'll shoot my way out if I have to. But first I need money; every cent you keep in that safe of yours.'

Gubby didn't bother to protest; he wasn't even wearing a gun. If he made some lame excuse about not having the key, he knew that Darch was in the mood to pistol-whip him.

'I'll get you the money, Sheldon,' he said. 'I just hope you can spend it in Hell!'

Darch watched him take a key out of his waistcoat pocket and walk over to the wall-safe. The door swung open to reveal a bundle of bank-notes, but then Darch realized that the saloon-owner's hand was straying even deeper into the safe's interior...

Downstairs in the bar of the saloon nothing had changed. After receiving the warning from Sheldon Darch, Corbett didn't take his eyes off the solitary card-player for a single second. Likewise, the other hired gun, Stiles, kept a watchful eye on the deputy marshal, waiting for him to make a move. Billy Eason prayed that Luke wouldn't do anything rash; if trouble exploded now there was no guarantee they could outdraw the seasoned gunfighters facing them.

Billy was watching for a sign from his partner, a movement of the hand or a jerk of the head. Instead, a shot rang out on the floor above their heads and the whole situation changed in a moment.

Startled by the shot, Corbett's head jerked round towards the staircase, giving Luke the chance to leap to his feet and draw his .45. Luke fired, but without taking proper aim, and his slug merely brought the wall mirror crashing down behind the counter. Corbett swung back round to meet the danger. His draw was smooth, but he was unlucky when his bullet embedded itself in the edge of the table where Luke had been sitting. Luke took full advantage of his good fortune; his second shot sent Corbett staggering back against the counter. The gunslinger tried to aim a second time, but the life was oozing out of him and he sank helplessly on to the sawdust floor.

Stiles was also caught unawares by the shooting upstairs, and even more so by the violent duel between Corbett and the card-player, who was a stranger to him. Instinctively, Stiles went for his gun, but before he could level it Billy Eason was on him like a wildcat. Billy's mission was to arrest at least one of Hank Morris's killers. He pinned Stiles's arms to his sides and wrestled him to the floor.

As they fell Billy felt the shock waves as Stiles's Colt exploded. Then Stiles started screaming and thrashing about. Billy disentangled himself and seized the gun that was now lying by the gunslinger's side. Stiles was out of the fight. His own slug had shot away half his boot and half of his left foot had gone with it.

Billy turned Stiles's gun on the bartender,

in case the fellow got any ideas about inter-
vening in the fight. However, the bartender
merely held up his hands open-palmed as if
to say: I only work here. Meanwhile, Luke
was on his way up the broad staircase.

Sheldon Darch was stuffing Loyd Gubby's
bank-notes inside his shirt when he heard
the opening shots of the gun battle
downstairs. His former employer was lying
lifeless on the rich carpet at his feet. Darch
was by no means triumphant; he had a long
way to go, and he knew it. He just hoped
that Corbett and Stiles were removing some
of the obstacles in his path.

He soon learned otherwise. When he left
the room he found someone waiting for him
at the far end of the passageway. It was his
old enemy from the Double D ranch. Luke's
Colt was already out of its holster, but Darch
drew his own .45 with arrogant ease and
shot the Colt from Luke's numbed fingers.

As Luke crouched there, nursing his hand,
Darch strode up to him and told him
contemptuously:

'Don't worry, cowboy, I ain't gonna kill you. You're my ticket out of this town. Get moving.'

At the head of the staircase Billy Eason froze when he saw Luke moving towards him crab-fashion, propelled by the barrel of Sheldon Darch's Colt.

'Drop the gun, Mister Deputy,' Darch said, 'or I'll kill your partner.'

Billy hesitated; Darch was holding all the cards, but he knew he'd be committing suicide if he threw away his six-gun. Sheldon Darch aimed the Colt at the side of Luke's head to show that he meant what he said.

'Do like he says, Billy,' Luke yelled. 'Drop the gun, damn you, drop the gun!'

Billy thought suddenly of Mary Stoller and Sandra Drake. If he was the cause of Luke's death their lives would never be the same again – and neither would his. He dropped the gun.

Master of the situation, Sheldon Darch swung the Colt around to cover Billy Eason.

'I only need one of you,' he remarked with

a thin smile. 'No hard feelings.'

As Billy Eason stared death in the face, a sharp crack rang out. A small hole opened up in Darch's forehead and his face registered pain and astonishment. He rocked back and forth for a moment or two before his legs gave way and brought him crashing to the ground.

Billy stared as the derringer disappeared from Luke's hand just as quickly as it had appeared. It was a little while before either of them spoke. Then,

'I thought you told your pa the pastor no more tricks,' Billy Eason commented with mock severity.

Luke's fingers were still stinging from his encounter with the gunslinger, but he managed to raise a smile when he replied.

'Well, maybe once in a while, Billy,' he said. 'Just to keep my hand in!'

The publishers hope that this book has given you enjoyable reading. Large Print Books are especially designed to be as easy to see and hold as possible. If you wish a complete list of our books please ask at your local library or write directly to:

Dales Large Print Books
Magna House, Long Preston,
Skipton, North Yorkshire.
BD23 4ND